Dead Sexy

Two Tales of Vampire Erotica

Also by Kim Corum:

Playtime
99 Martinis: Uncensored
Heartbreaker
Breaking the Girl
The Other Woman
Now She's Gone
Eager to Please

Dead Sexy

Two Tales of Vampire Erotica

by

Kim Corum

New Tradition Books

Dead Sexy: Two Tales of Vampire Erotica
by
Kim Corum

New Tradition Books
ISBN 193242055X
All rights reserved
Copyright © 2006 by Kim Corum
This book may not be reproduced in whole or in part without written permission.

This book is a work of fiction. Names, characters, places and incidents are either the product of the author's imagination or are used fictitiously. Any resemblance to actual events or locales or persons, living or dead is entirely coincidental.

For information contact:
New Tradition Books
newtraditionbooks@yahoo.com

For my favorite bloodsucker.

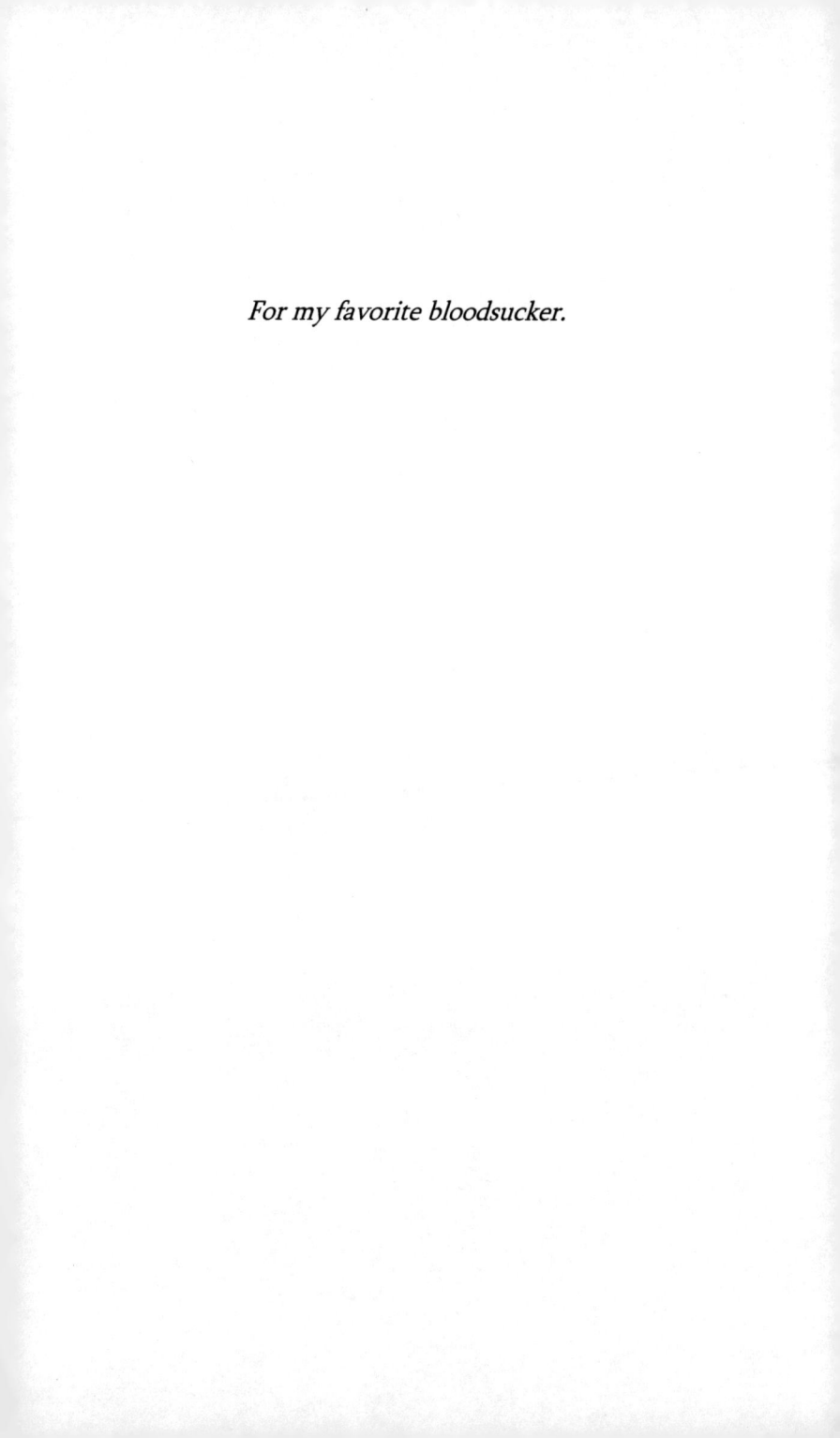

Book one.

Breathe

Cravings.

The hunt was the least favorite part of the night. For me, I mean. Hugo loved it. But then again, he'd come to love it as any normal vampire would. It's just that I wasn't a normal vampire.

Hugo and I sat at the bar and waited for the victim to arrive. It was getting late and we were both starving. The red wine glasses were almost empty and the bartender was getting tired. The crowd was thinning out and Hugo was getting slightly agitated. But then he was horny too. He always got so horny and alive before a kill.

I tried not to think about that.

I tried not to think about that as I felt his hand move up my arm and then push the hair away from my neck before his lips came to rest on the skin just below my ear. He gave me a long, slow kiss before pulling away, standing and then walking off. His hand came out towards me and I stood, taking it as I stared at the man in the booth who I knew was going to be our victim. He was an older man and he was staring at us intently. He was wondering what it would be like to be Hugo, who, he was sure, was taking me home to fuck me.

I stared at the man as I walked out, stared at him until he looked into my eyes. And once he did, he immediately rose and followed us. We walked slowly, with purpose, out the door and onto the street. I turned around to see the man following closely at our heels. I turned back around and held fast to Hugo's hand. He squeezed my hand then ducked into an alley as I walked on.

I never heard or saw a thing.

I walked about a block, then turned back around and went back to the alley. Hugo nodded at me and I got on my knees next to the man, who was now only barely alive. I avoided his heavy-lidded eyes and the sun spots on his hands. I didn't think about who this man was or the children—and grandchildren—he might have. Hugo went in for the blood that would feed me. I didn't watch as he did it. But as soon as he turned to me, I opened my mouth and the man's blood trickled in. Once I felt that rush of blood, of life, a sense of calm and purpose came over me.

Hugo kept doing this until I was full. Then he finished the man off. When he was done, he stood, took my hand and we walked away.

This was the way it was. This was the way it had been for a while. But all that was about to change.

"Do you know how truly beautiful you are, Lola?" he asked me later that night.

I nodded and smiled a little. He made me feel so beautiful that it didn't embarrass me to agree. I felt no shame from the compliment. I never felt shame around him—ever. My hair was long and dark and my eyes were blue, crystal clear blue. My skin was subtle and as undamaged as a baby's. My body was ripe for the taking, small and delicate, petite but with a nice ass and a great set of breasts, which he loved to devour.

"You are," he said, staring at me. "You are truly beautiful."

Book one.

Breathe

Through the eyes of our lovers, we see time. We see ourselves standing in it, standing in time, being ourselves and being loved for just that. That is what we crave. That's the way I saw him, for who he really was. That's the way he said he saw me. Innocent but hurt, craving something. He wanted to give me that something I needed that neither of us could name.

"You don't fool me," I told him once. "You're evil."

"That I am, love," he said, giving me a sheepish grin. "But then again, so are you."

And I was. Evil. It was strange to say, strange to be, evil. But I was evil. I was as evil as he was. He had made me that way. He had destroyed me, only to bring me back from the dead, to the living. That's where I was now. Before him, I'd not been myself, not been the person or thing I was supposed to be. I had always been alone, unfulfilled. He had made me feel, he had made me full. He made me into the thing I was now. I was finally whole.

And now he was giving me that look again. That look that told me it was time to submit and to allow him to take me over. It was time, the look said, for me to lie down and take what he was going to give. I tensed in anticipation, tensed almost with fear. Our love making was always violent, despite the fact that it could be sweet and controlled. We liked it rough, though, and when we were done, we would survey the marks on our bodies that would heal almost as soon as they appeared. We would be proud of the marks, proud of our insatiable appetite for each other. Proud that we could bring that animal out.

The sex was the best I'd ever had in my entire life. It was addicting, the sex, and the more I had, the more I wanted. It was more fun in the beginning, when he didn't look so remorseful.

Sometimes, he would tie me up just to let me go. I would lie there and anticipate his next move. I would lie there and watch him watching me. He loved to stare at me, at my naked body. He loved to hold back and make me squirm, make me beg for it. And I'd beg. I'd do anything to get it. That's how good it made me feel. It made me feel so good I'd act like a fool, like a complete fool, just to have it again, just to feel him so close to me. He made me feel so alive, so free, so uninhibited, so insatiable. All the things in the world I'd been missing before I met him, I felt. I felt them so much I sometimes wondered how I used to feel and that emptiness would always threaten to fill me again. But as long as he made me feel like this, as long as he stayed around, I'd be okay. I'd be fine as long as he made me feel like I was meant to feel.

Just as he was making me feel now.

Now he was all mine. He was giving me the look. The look told me I was the sexiest creature he'd ever come in contact with. The look told me he wasn't going to move one inch until I gave him the signal.

"Go ahead," I said. "Do it."

He grinned at me. I smiled back from my position on the bed, which I was tied to. I couldn't move. Well, I could have if I had wanted to. I was strong, so strong that I never had to find myself in a position where I had to submit to anyone. I could tug at the rope just a little and it'd break. I could get away if I wanted to. But I didn't want to. All I wanted to do was tell him what I wanted and what I wanted was to be fucked. Fucked good.

He bent over me, over my naked body, and ran his head up and down it, nuzzling me. I began to feel it, to feel warm. This was the best part, the anticipation. Without it, I couldn't go on to do the things we were going to do.

He began to run his hands over my body, stopping to fondle my breasts. I rose up from the bed at that, wanting his lips on my nipples, wanting him on top of me. But not so soon. He kept his hands moving as he stared at me from the corner of his eye. He was watching me again. He loved to watch.

"What now?" he asked softly.

"Touch me," I said. "Touch me there."

"Where?" he asked and slid his hand between my legs. "There?"

I squeezed my eyes shut and nodded. It felt so good as he touched and explored me down there. No inch was left uncovered, undiscovered. He moved his hand a little and found my spot. I moaned loudly and licked my lips. It was too much, it was too good. I had to have it, though. I would have died if I didn't.

His hand stayed still and I began to move against it, using it to get off, to come. He bent down and nibbled at me, licking and pushing his head between my legs. My legs began to part and invited him in to taste me. So he did. He tasted me, licked at me and within seconds, I was erupting with pleasure, with orgasm, with pure and total delight.

Then he was on top of me, kissing me, giving me himself. As he kissed me, I began to respond and kiss back, harder, wanting him inside of me. His mouth found my nipple and began to suck greedily at it, grabbing at it and squeezing as he gave me pleasure. I wished my hands were free to explore him, so I jerked on the ropes and they broke, leaving my hands untied. My arms encircled him and squeezed tight. He moaned as my hands went down his back and to his ass and there they squeezed. My hands came back up and held his head still so I could kiss him and lick at his lips.

His lips ate at mine as if he were starving. And he was. He was starving with lust for me. He couldn't get enough of my lips or of me. I loved having that power over him to bring him to the point of no return.

"Now," I said, looking into his eyes. "Do it now."

Without a word, he complied and pushed my legs open with his knee. His body settled between my legs and I felt his hard cock on my leg before I felt it pushing inside of me.

I moaned as soon as he was all the way in. We were complete now, two pieces to the puzzle, solved. We were one together, one alone, one person, one being, and one thing. It was just me and him, us against the world, us alone in ours.

His mouth was back on top of mine as he began to fuck me, take me over, control me. I sucked at his lips, loving the way his skin felt against mine. Then we began to move together, move as one. Our eyes opened and we stared intensely at one another, almost smiling. This is what we liked best. It was the best in us, giving it to each other.

He began to fuck me, really fuck me, which sent me over the edge, which made me beg and moan for him to do it, to do it harder, to take me, to ravish me. He loved doing this to me. He knew it drove me crazy, wild. I loved having it done to me. I loved fucking him. I loved him, it was that simple.

It took us over then. We were only participants, caught up in the mood, in the love. We were overcome with passion and all we could do was hang on and ride it out. Our eyes were filled with lust for one another and our loins craved each other. There was nothing left to do but come and come we did. We came hard, slamming into each other, taking what we could and consuming it greedily. I was panting and I was shivering with delight and then I was done.

So was he.

We didn't say a word afterwards. There wasn't really much we could have said. The intensity of it spoke for itself. He only settled on the bed beside me and took me in his arms. He stared into my eyes before he touched the side of my face with his hand.

"You know I love you, right?" he asked.

I smiled and said, "And I love you, too."

He nodded, kissed my cheek and then closed his eyes. I stared at the window. It was morning, daylight, and it was time for rest. I closed my eyes, too.

✷ ✷ ✷ ✷ ✷

It was still daylight when I opened my eyes the next day. I never awoke during the day and therefore, I immediately knew that something was wrong. My intuition was buzzing, telling me to get up and see what was going on. And I knew something was wrong because the bedroom door was wide open and there were no lights on in the living room which was darkened—almost to the point of pitch black—by heavy curtains to keep out the sunlight. There was also no noise from the TV. He always kept the TV on. He was usually up before me, hours before me, and, as he waited for me to wake, he watched it to pass the time. He didn't sleep as much as me.

Why wasn't the TV on?

I got up and looked around the room, then went out to the living room. "Hugo? You there?"

But I knew he wasn't there. The room was too still.

I went into the kitchen and wondered what was going on. *His coat!* I ran out to the hall closet and threw the door open. Hugo's coat was gone. The hanger where it usually hung swung from the breeze of the door being opened. The only coat that was in there was mine. It looked lonely.

I went into the bathroom and noticed all his stuff was gone from there, too. His toothpaste and toothbrush. His razor. And inside of the closet, his favorite clothes were also gone. When did he pack them? How did he do it without me seeing him? When I was asleep? While I was in the shower? Gone to the corner market? When? When did all this happen?

I went back into the living room to look for some evidence, for something to let me know that I wasn't just freaking out for no good reason. I didn't find anything. No note, no nothing. Nothing but stillness, a quiet apartment, an empty room. It was so quiet and still in there, I couldn't stand it.

He was gone and I knew it. And I also knew he hadn't just gone for a newspaper or a cup of coffee. He was gone for good. And I knew he'd gone last night, right after I'd fallen asleep. He'd gone in the darkness, creeping away like the creature of the night he was.

That's when I noticed the note. It was on the coffee table, half-tucked into one of the old books he liked to read. My hands shook as I picked it up. I knew what it would say before I opened it and it said, "I'm gone. Don't try to find me."

I'm gone. Don't try to find me.

So it was true. He was gone. And he didn't want to be found. I felt all this intense emotion well up inside of me. I felt sick with it, as though I could vomit. I felt my heart break and die a thousand deaths. Then I began to panic. What was I going to do without him? I couldn't live without him! I had to have him to feed me. I would die without him. No, I wouldn't die. I would shrivel up and become skin and bones with no heartbeat. I'd be a thing, lying there on the floor until someone came by and swept me away.

I fell back onto the couch and burst into tears. This wasn't the way it was supposed to turn out. Why did it have to turn out like this? I wiped the tears away with the back of my hand, then realized I was staring directly at the scars on my wrists.

"Tell me what it felt like," he said once, grabbing my wrist and staring at it. "All that good blood gone to waste."

I pulled it back in embarrassment.

"Why did you do it?" he asked.

"What?" I snapped.

"Try to kill yourself."

"Who says I did?" I asked.

"You did," he said. "And you didn't do it right, either."

I cringed.

"Tell me why," he said, coming up behind me, whispering in my ear. "Tell me why you wanted to die."

Because I was numb, so numb. Not afraid, just numb. I had wanted to feel something sometime. It felt as though I never would again. I turned to him. "How did you know?"

"The scars," he said. "They told me."

I stared at the scars, the ones that would never heal, even after I was turned. These scars, the ones on my wrists, were the only scars on my body that hadn't vanished. They stayed around to remind me that I'd been more dead in my previous life than I was in this one.

"Tell me why you did it," he said. "I want to know."

I shrugged. I don't know why I had tried to kill myself that time. All I can remember was standing in the shower and feeling so numb, the way depression makes a person feel. It felt like I was in a big, black hole filled with water. It felt like I was submerged and I'd never be able to surface. I stood there and stood there and willed myself to feel something. I didn't and I got pissed off. I got out of the shower and stomped into the kitchen, grabbed a steak knife and then… Then I cut myself. Once, then twice. The blood flowed but it didn't pour. It didn't gush the way I'd expected it to gush. It merely trickled. I stared down at the blood dripping from my wrist and began to panic. But at least I felt something. I felt silly and stupid.

Maybe I did it for pity. But I didn't tell anyone and I hoped no one would find out. I had wrapped my wrists up and ran to the hospital, praying I wouldn't die before I got there. I was so ashamed of myself.

"But why?" he asked. "Why did you do it?"

I stared at him and said honestly, "I needed to feel something and I thought that was the only way. I took it overboard, though."

He nodded slightly. "And why did you think you had to do it?"

"Because I was depressed," I muttered. "Because I wanted something I'd lost."

"And what had you lost?"

"Myself."

And now I was all alone, once again, feeling that same panic, feeling like I'd lost myself again. It felt odd to be so alone in this big, over-populated world but that's what I was. With him, with Hugo, I had been with someone, I had felt like somebody. Now I was back to being a nobody. Why did he have to take that away from me?

Hugo, where are you, baby?

Why did I have to give myself to him in the first place? What a fool I'd been to do that, to just throw away my heart with wild abandon. But that's what love does to people, it turns them into fools. You can hold on tight and never let it go but once you give it away you can never get it back. And I'd given it away. There was no way to get it back. I'd given it away to Hugo.

Hugo, Hugo, Hugo. As old as the hills. So old that he still spelled vampire with a "y", instead of an "i"—vampyre. Hugo, so old the accent of his youth was only barely there. What old country did he originate from? He never told me. I asked once and he said, "What does it matter?" I had blushed because it mattered to me. I think he came from Wales, though he never confirmed it.

Hugo, so old but so young, as young at heart as a child. As happy as lark. As handsome as the handsomest man alive. As intriguing as the night and as frightening as a really scary movie. Hugo with the dark hair and the dark blue eyes. Hugo who was born centuries ago, way before most of the history I'd studied in school.

Sometimes he could be mean, cruel. Sometimes he would yell at me, demand to know what was wrong with me. I didn't know. I didn't know what was wrong with me nor did I know how to control it. I wanted to be like him, just like him, but it wasn't in me. The thought of his rage at me, at all the cruel and heartless things he'd said to me, angered me now. How could he do this to me? I deserved better. He turned me and then he left me. Why?

"Why did you leave me?" I whispered, calling out to him. I could do that, I could call to him and he would hear me. Maybe he would listen. But, no, nothing. I heard nothing. Had he turned himself off to me?

I looked around the apartment. This had been our ninth or tenth place. It was in New York City, near Soho. This was my favorite place we'd lived. Before we'd lived in New Orleans, Los Angeles, Chicago. We'd lived all over the United States. We'd lived in the dark where no one could see us. But then who needs the day? You can do the same things at night as you can during daylight. Sometimes more.

I got up and went to the closet in the bedroom and began to dress. It would be a while before I could go out, but soon, I'd be able to start the hunt. Soon, I'd come face to face with him again and I'd demand to know why he'd left. But I knew why. But I didn't want to think about that just yet.

He might leave me but he wasn't leaving me without telling me why. I wanted to hear it come from his lips, from out of his mouth. I was going to find him and once I did, I was going to ask him to explain. I would listen to what he had to say and I wouldn't interrupt.

And then what? Then what would I do? What could I do? I thought about it and thought about it. And then I realized what I would do, what I'd have to do in order to survive. I'd kill him. It was the only way to neutralize the situation. Wasn't that the way it worked? Hadn't I heard that? If you kill the one who made you, you go back to being human? Most vampires wouldn't do it because, by the time they caught up to the vampire who'd made them, they'd be so old it would age them, sometimes to the point of death. I'd age ten years older in one heartbeat. I had only been twenty-six when he'd turned me. I'd be thirty-six when it was over. Maybe nothing at all would happen, but it was worth a try. It wouldn't be the same as killing a human; I'd be killing something evil. I'd be killing something I loved.

I put my head in my hands and thought about it. It was the only way, to kill him. I hated the thought, but we'd been through so much it was the only way for me to have a chance. Without him around, I'd wither away from hunger but I wouldn't die. Without the mercy of dying, I would be too weak to live and too immortal to die. It would be absolute hell.

It'd be hard to find him, to track him. It'd be hard to put a stake through his heart. But then again, it'd be hard to wither away, too.

I could do it. I could kill him. I could handle that. But I couldn't handle being left. I'd been left before, once before.

My husband had left me, leaving a note on the kitchen table like the coward he'd been. Leaving a note telling me I hadn't been good enough, I'd been too much trouble, too depressing to be around. He'd left me and I'd found Hugo, which had made the world a better place. And he was gone too. And now I had to find him and I had to kill him. I had to do it. It was the only way to make me human again. If I couldn't be a vampire with him, I'd be a human without him. It was the only way to get my breath back and once I did that, I could breathe again.

My vampyre.

At first I was scared, then I wasn't. At first I hesitated, then chastised myself for my fear. This was what I wanted. He was what I needed. I'd do anything I had to in order to get it. I knew he'd never do me any real harm. How I knew, I don't know, but I *knew*.

I can still remember it like it was yesterday. The day it happened, the time on the alarm clock on the nightstand. I can remember the determined look in his eyes, as if he'd done this before—and he had—and knew exactly how to do it. I can remember the anticipation and the exhilaration. I can remember the way we danced afterwards and the warmth that filled my cold heart and gave it a new life.

"Are you sure?" he's said. "Tell me you're sure."

"I'm sure."

And I was. I was ready for him to do it. Even in the moment when he came at me, I wanted it. I never backed down. I begged for it. I begged him to do it. I wanted relief from the world I was in, from the loneliness in my heart. I wanted him to give it to me.

He did.

It happened so suddenly. All I felt was the sharpness of his teeth sinking into my neck and then I blacked out, only to come to a moment later a totally changed and different being. One moment I was alive and the next I was dead. But I'd never felt more alive. He made me feel real even though he took away everything I had. He saved me from my own worst enemy—myself. He saved me from the nothing I was, always had been before I met him.

He took my breath away and I could no longer breathe. He'd stolen my heartbeat, my life, my soul. He took it all away and replaced it with his own. We became one in that moment, the moment where he simultaneously destroyed me and gave me life. He gave me life to this—to this killer, this demon, this vampire. To this thing I was. To what I had become. To what I begged to become.

Now he was gone. And I knew why he'd left. It mostly had to do with the same reason my husband had left—I wasn't good enough. It was hard never being good enough for anyone, not human nor vampire.

None of that mattered now. Nothing mattered but getting my breath back and that's what he had been, my breath, my reason for living. Now he was my enemy, my prey.

I was ready now. I was just waiting until it was time. I sat on the couch and waited for it to get dark outside. As I waited, he came to me. I didn't try to block him out. He crept into my mind and told me he wanted me. He still wanted me, after all this time. He told me to keep it up, not to give up on myself. He was sorry but this was just how it had to be.

I shook my head and turned him off. But he was coming on strong, trying to take over my mind. It was almost like the first time we met, when he'd started to hunt me. Back then, I knew if he would just leave me alone, I could alter my destination and my purpose. But he wouldn't. He kept at me until I was under his control, until he had me. Now, he was still there; he was still teasing me, teasing me from afar, making me want him still.

"Shut up!" I yelled.

"You know why," he said. "You know why I left."

I squeezed my eyes shut and shook my head.

"Don't try to find me," he said.

And then he was gone, though he was still there in my mind. And he was gone because I wasn't good enough to be a vampire like him. I was nothing, really. I wasn't human and I wasn't a vampire. Technically, I was both, but then again, I was neither. I'd never transitioned into being a full-blown vampire. I couldn't kill but I could feed off the blood of others as long as someone—Hugo—did it for me. It was that simple and that was my deep, dark secret. I was less than human, less than vampire. I was caught in-between two worlds, swaying with need and hunger. It was like part of myself was missing and he was the missing link. The one I needed, the one I had to have in order to survive.

"Hugo," I said aloud. "Why did you leave me?"

He didn't answer. He used to always answer me. We could hear each other even if we were miles and miles apart. I could feel the blood beating in his heart and I could feel him breathe on the back of my neck. But he didn't have breath and his heart didn't beat. That's what he'd stolen from me, my breath and then my heart. I could not breathe without him and I could not live without my heart. Without him, I would suffocate. He wasn't far from me now. But I would gain on him. And once I found him...

I shook my head and got up and went to the window. It was getting dark. Soon, I'd be able to go out and look for him. I had my plan. I would sleep all day and rise at night to hunt him. I'd follow his scent and keep myself hot on his trail and then I'd find him. He'd be crafty. But he couldn't hide from me for very long. We were too close to one another, too alike. He was playing cat and mouse. He thought he was the cat but we both knew he was the mouse.

"Lola," he called to me once. "Little Lola."

"It's Louise," I said.

"It should be Lola," he told me.

And so it was. He'd even renamed me, taken my name and shortened it. That was alright. Anything the bastard wanted to do was alright by me. Besides abandoning me.

I stared out the window at all of them, at all the people on the street below me. They were like little ants on the street, scurrying under the darkening and rainy sky. All hurrying home to their home-cooked meals and problems. All hurrying home so they could get up and do it all over tomorrow. I had once been just like them. I'd been worse than they had been. I had been a bitter divorcée with a load of baggage. I'd been a lonely girl in a southern city—New Orleans. How like Hugo to pick a girl from New Orleans to turn. He loved that city, loved its darkness.

"No matter what you do to New Orleans," he said once. "No matter how many tourists visit, no matter how friendly it gets, there will always be a certain darkness to it. And that's what draws everyone here."

I stared at him, knowing exactly what he meant.

"You are like this city," he whispered in my ear. "You have darkness inside of you but it's hidden by the light."

I knew what he meant by that, too. I was a pretty woman, I was nice, and people liked me. But they didn't know me. They didn't know that underneath all the smiles and politeness was a person who felt unsafe and unsure of herself. They didn't know about the dark depression, either. They didn't know me at all. And I had all of them fooled.

I had been a mess, a neurotic mess. I had problems by the load. I hated myself and my position in life. I thought I'd never love again and that my divorce had destroyed my heart. I had been wrong. To Hugo I was ripe for the taking. For the eating.

I dreamed of him before we met, long before he turned me into what I had become. He came to me at night and played inside my head. I knew his voice, his faint Welsh accent. I knew the curve of his hand and I knew the distinct color of blue that his eyes were. I knew about the lock of dark hair that fell over his eyes when he laughed. I had dreamed about him for nights, night after night. It was only after he turned me that he told me he'd sat outside my window and watched me sleep. He'd put himself into my dreams. He had made me want him. He had picked me, he said, out of the crowd.

"And why wouldn't I?" he whispered behind me.

I shivered as he lifted my arms above my head so he could remove my shirt.

"So beautiful," he said. "So alone. So like me."

The shirt fell on the floor and his hands were on my stomach and then on my breasts. He touched the nipples and began to softly kiss the back of my neck. I shuddered with delight as he began to eat at me, as his mouth began to suck at my neck.

"Oh, I would love to devour you," he whispered. "Would you like that?"

"Mmm," I moaned and turned to him so he could kiss me. He took me over with his mouth, sliding his tongue in and out just so that I wanted more and more. I pressed my body up next to his.

"I could make you whole again, Lola," he muttered.

"Yes," I moaned. "Make me whole again."

He walked me back to the bed and pushed me down. I laid there and anticipated his touch. I laid there and wanted him on top of me, inside of me, giving me everything he had. I wanted to take it all and then ask for more.

His hands were all over my body, caressing me, waking me up. That was the first time we'd make love and the last. Later on, we would only fuck, taking that lust we had for one another and devouring it. But right now he was giving me what a woman wants most—the feeling of being totally and utterly wanted by her lover—and what he was giving I was willing to die for.

His hands were sliding between my thighs and I moaned and began to tingle down there, down between my legs. I wanted his lips and mouth there and they were, sucking on me so hard I was nearly convulsing with pleasure. He played with me as he sucked, sliding his fingers in and out and then rubbing my spot until I was shaking with orgasm and as soon as I came, he was on top of me, bearing down into me. He was having me, taking me and I was giving it back, giving him all I had and begging him to take more.

And he did. He took me then, easing his big cock into me, filling me up and taking me over. He held still and made me work for it, made me beg for him to move. And I did. I begged until he was ramming inside of me. I felt whole then, as if nothing in the world would ever matter but that moment. And nothing had. We came together, each of us moaning with this intense pleasure. As we came down from the orgasm, we stared at each other and we knew neither of us would ever be the same.

It was love. We didn't speak it, but it was love. It was love we both felt, love that we both needed. We were both willing to give it to the other.

The next day, he showed me what he was. He didn't tell me. No, that wasn't his style. He showed me. We were in the Quarter drinking and I was so happy, so happy that my heart was opening up again. So happy to be with him. He made me so high I could have spread my arms and flown like a bird.

But what exactly did he see in me? Easy prey? No. he saw something no one else could. He saw a woman who he thought would stand by his side and ease his loneliness.

"Eternity," he said once. "Is highly overrated. And boring, too. Unless you have someone with you, what's the point?"

But that night, we were passing by an alley and an old man, a bum, was sitting beside a trashcan. He called out to Hugo, asking for his spare change. Hugo got a mischievous look in his eye and the next thing I knew, he was sucking the life out of the old man.

I just stood there, unable to fathom what was going on. Then I began to scream. He glared at me and I saw his teeth. He was a monster. I didn't know what type, but I knew he was a monster. I found myself running away from him. He let me get a few blocks away, then he was beside me grabbing my arm and pulling me into a darkened doorway.

"Well," he said. "What do you think?"

"You're a monster!" I screamed.

He nodded. "And you're going to be just like me."

Problem was, he was dead wrong about that.

But I wasn't about to give up the search before it began. I would chase him. He'd probably be just out of my reach. But I would gain on him. Nothing was going to stop me. Nothing was going to stand in my way.

I sighed and was about to pull back from the window when I noticed a small child walking with his mother. He had a ball and he tried to walk and bounce it at the same time. The ball got away from him and he and his mother ran over to it. The mother grabbed it and handed it to him. The child smiled, then giggled. I realized that I would never feel that joy again, that sense of life. It was all dead inside me.

I felt a hopelessness so overwhelming I wanted to burst into tears. We're not supposed to cry. We're evil creatures. We're vile and we take life without thought. But that was the problem. I wasn't any more evil than I'd been when I was human. If I was, he might not have left me.

✭ ✭ ✭ ✭ ✭

You wear black to slip into the shadows and that's what you do, you slip into the shadows. You're not part of anything and you're totally alone. That's the way it was and that's what I did when I went out that night.

I sensed Hugo was somewhere in the Village. It wouldn't be like Hugo to leave the city right away. He'd wait until later, when he could feed, then he'd sneak away. I swept through the Village, then back again, catching his scent once. I followed it to the subway and then I lost it. I cursed and was about to go back out onto the street when someone caught my eye. Or some *thing* rather.

I turned just in time to see something in a long green overcoat hop off the platform and disappear. I looked around. No one else had seen it. That's the way it usually worked. But, being a vampire, I could recognize things humans couldn't. I followed it, jumping down onto the tracks and hurrying before it got out of my sight.

This was what I liked best about being a vampire. I was fearless. Before I wouldn't even have ridden the subway by myself but now I was following something down into the underbelly of the city. I was strong and I liked that. I loved having no fear.

I finally made it to what appeared to be a maintenance area. I heard a scuffle and turned to see the thing disappear into a tunnel of some sort. I raced after it, crawling on my belly until I reached the end of the tunnel and there I fell out of it and onto a big pile of trash.

The thing was on me immediately. I almost laughed. He was no match for me. In one quick motion, I caught his throat with my elbow. He limped away from me, holding it.

"What the hell did you do that for?" he asked.

"I don't like to be touched," I said and eyed him. He was short and he was ugly and he was covered in warts. "What are you?"

"A troll," he said and massaged his throat. "And I can kill you."

"Sure, whatever," I said and looked around at the place which was covered in filth. "What is this? Your hovel?"

"Now don't be coming in here making fun of my place," he said in a huff. "Just what the fuck do you want?"

"I'm looking for someone," I said.

He nodded and coughed. "He isn't here."

"You don't even know who I'm talking about."

"Hugo?" he said and threw his arms up. "He was here already. He came sometime yesterday, then today too."

Damn it. I stared at the thing. He wasn't lying. "What did he want with you?"

"Same thing all you vamps want," he said and threw me a bottle.

I held it up. It was filled with some green fluid. "What is this?"

"Troll blood," he said.

"*Eww!*" I screeched and threw it to the side where it landed on top of an old pile of clothes.

He shook his head at me and picked it up. "Fine. I thought you might want some, too."

"What does it do?"

"Supposedly, you drink this and you can go out in the sun for a day."

I grabbed it back and then glared at him. "What do you mean 'supposedly'?"

"Alright, it works," he said and sat down in an old recliner. "Now that's twenty bucks."

"It's not worth twenty bucks," I said and put it in my coat pocket. "Why did he want this?"

He shrugged. "Listen, lady, I don't know. He came in here same as you and I sold him some. End of story."

"Do you know where he went?"

"He mentioned something about Cleveland," he said.

"Cleveland?" I asked. "What's there? A special place for vampires or something?"

"No," he said. "Rock and Roll Hall of Fame."

I rolled my eyes and started out of the hovel.

"Why do you want him?" he asked, turning in his seat to watch me walk out.

"Because I'm going to kill him."

"Oh," he called after me. "Good luck with that. Wait! You forgot to pay me."

I threw him a twenty and left.

Eternal love.

It was supposed to be fun. It was supposed to be what I was always meant to be. But then it wasn't fun and it was black and evil and all the things children—and some adults—get scared about.

"Her," Hugo said and pointed at the young woman. "She'll be your first."

I stared at her and blinked. She was dancing in the club as if she were alone in her bedroom, in front of a mirror. But she wasn't alone. She was in big crowd of other dancers. She was in the middle of it all. She was so totally unaware of herself, it almost made me jealous. She was so pretty, so alive and daring. Everyone in the club stared at her too, at her beauty, her vivaciousness. I was nothing like her. Sure, we shared beauty but I wasn't as outgoing. I wondered briefly why Hugo chose me instead of someone like her. I also wondered when I'd get some of that vampire confidence I so desperately needed. It was just like Hugo to choose someone like her and not the wallflower of the club. I didn't know if I could do it.

"Take her," he said.

I couldn't move. I knew I had to but I couldn't.

"Go on now," he said. "I'll watch you."

"Here?" I asked.

"Yes, here," he said. "Go up to her and get her to dance with you."

"How can I do that?"

He turned my face to his and stared into my eyes. "Your eyes. Make contact with her eyes. She will become mesmerized. She'll do whatever you want."

He was right. He'd mesmerized me the first night we'd met.

He nudged me. "Go on now."

I got up and began to make my way to the dancefloor, to her. I felt the music. A good electonica song played and I moved to the beat as I made my way over. She noticed me immediately and smiled. I smiled back, careful not to reveal my slightly longer than normal incisor teeth. She and I began to dance. I moved in closer to her and breathed her smell in. She smelled divine, like she would taste so good. And I was so hungry. Hugo hadn't fed me since he'd turned me, almost three days before.

She was taller than I was and I had to stare up at her. She stared at me and smiled again, then leaned over and yelled over the music, "I'm Elizabeth!"

Elizabeth. Elizabeth? Her name was Elizabeth. I had a sudden vision of her mother giving birth to her. Then I had a vision of her playing with dolls as a young child and graduating high school. I had a vision of her first boyfriend and then a vision of her small apartment furnished with old furniture her family had given her.

I shook the vision out of my head and tried to concentrate. But something was stopping me. I was getting hot and panicky. I felt odd. I felt so odd.

Someone started dancing behind me. It was Hugo. He pressed in close to me, kissed my neck, and then pushed me in closer to Elizabeth before whispering, "Kiss her before you bite."

But I had no desire. The desire just didn't come. I didn't want to do it, even though I was so ravenous I could eaten a whole village. The music got louder. It was pounding in my head. I thought my head was going to explode.

"Do it," he hissed. "Now before she suspects something!"

Elizabeth was staring at both of us with a slight smile on her face. Maybe she was thinking about having sex with us in a big bed. Maybe she was thinking about getting a drink at the bar. I don't know what she was thinking, but I had to make my move and I had to make it quick. And so I did. I grabbed her face and pulled her lips to mine. She gasped, but allowed me to kiss her lips before I pressed my face into her neck and opened my mouth. Then she moaned. I froze.

"Now," Hugo whispered. "Now. I'll carry her out for you. No one will know."

Now—do it now! I opened my mouth to bite her and just as I did, a feeling of nausea came over me so strong that I almost passed out. I stumbled away from her.

"What are you doing?" Elizabeth said and stared at me with concern. "Are you okay?"

Before I could answer, Hugo took over and in once swift motion, overtook her. He stared into her eyes until she stared back without fear or any other kind of emotion. He pushed her hair away from her neck and, in a second, devoured her, drinking her blood as everyone danced and danced. She shuddered and moaned, then shivered and gasped. It seemed to take forever for him to drain her, but soon she collapsed into his arms. He grabbed her up and carried her out. No one noticed. No one cared. Everyone thought they were playing or just getting ready to have some wild sex. No one knew she was dead.

I rushed out after them and found Hugo depositing her body in the alley next to the club. When I rushed up, he turned on me, his eyes flashing with rage. For a moment, I envisioned him hitting me. He didn't. I think he wanted to, though.

"You could have gotten us caught!" he roared. "What the fuck is wrong with you?"

"I don't know," I said. "I'll do better next time."

"You're damn right you will," he hissed and stomped off.

Problem was, I hadn't done better. And I never got that image of Elizabeth going down out of my mind.

I just missed Hugo in Cleveland, too. I dropped my head and got back in my car, ready to head out. He was headed south now, towards the Mason Dixon line. Where the hell was he going? And what was he doing?

I could only drive at night but since I had the troll's blood, I could have driven during the day, too. For one day. I should have made him give me more. I thought about drinking it and driving all night and into the next day. But for some reason, I thought it was best to save it. *You never know when you're going to need some troll's blood*, I thought. Then I laughed at the thought. Before Hugo, I would have never thought anything so ridiculous sounding.

And now it was almost dawn again. I'd have to get a room somewhere and hole up for the day. As I drove, I began to think about the night Hugo made me. How long it was, how I was so far from understanding the whole thing and the enormity of it.

"Let me go!" I had screamed.

He let me go. Since I lived near the Quarter, I began to walk home. He followed me.

"Leave me alone!" I yelled over my shoulder.

"At least let me make sure you get home okay."

I turned on him and said, "So you can kill me?"

Hugo stared at me and dropped his head. "Sorry. I thought you were different."

"Different how?" I snapped. "Different as in a killer?"

"I'm not a killer," he said. "I'm a vampire."

"Oh, please," I said. "You just… I mean… I…"

"What?" he asked softly. "What do you think you saw?"

I stopped and thought about it. What had I seen? I stared at him. He was really pale and was wearing all black. But that didn't mean anything. Artists tend to dress in all black, so do some women. I even had several all-black outfits. As far as I was concerned, he was just a creep, a murderer, someone who needed to go to jail. He was no more a vampire than I was. Vampires were made up, in stories. They didn't exist outside of movies and storybooks. They weren't real.

"I drained him," he said and grabbed my hand. "Listen, Lola, I can give you something no one in this world can give you. I can give you eternal life, eternal love."

I just stared at him. By that time, I was shaking with fear. I really thought he was going to kill me, too. I wished the police would have miraculously shown up right then and rescued me. If he didn't kill me, I was going to call them and he was going to jail, hopefully forever.

"I know how lonely you are," he whispered and stepped in closer to me. "I know how it feels. I know that when you wake up, you don't want to get out of bed because it's just another day of nothing. Am I right?"

I swallowed hard. He was hitting on something and he knew it. Sure, I was lonely but not lonely enough to let him turn me into a killer.

"I know that you cry at night," he told me. "I know that someone broke your heart and the world came crashing down on you. I know that your hopes and your dreams are all gone and you just exist from day to day. I can give you that light back in your life, Lola. I can give you everything you ever wanted."

"And what do you think I want?" I asked and stared him dead in the eye.

"Love."

He'd been right, that's what I had wanted, all I had ever dreamed about. Love, love and love. I wanted to be wanted. I needed that so bad. And he gave it to me. It scared me, the way he loved me. It was all-consuming, with complete abandon. When someone loves you like that it's hard not to want to run away, lest you get possessed. It's hard to lose yourself to that kind of love. But it's almost impossible to avoid.

So, of course, I had succumbed. Hugo got what he wanted—a vampire to spend his days with—and I had gotten what I wanted—eternal love.

"Yeah, right," I muttered and pulled off onto an off-ramp, wondering how to get the hell out of Cleveland. I didn't know where I was going or what I was doing. I needed to stop for a moment and gain some clarity. I realized I was in the industrial part of town where the streets were covered in grease and oil. It was deserted this late at night.

As I parked the car, I noticed something strange. There was a young woman walking alone. What the hell was she doing? I watched her make her way up the street as if she had no particular destination in mind. Was she a prostitute? Maybe her car had broken down. I watched her for a moment before I noticed that someone was following her. He was a tall man in dark clothing. He came up behind her very quickly. From the moment I laid eyes on him, I knew what he was. He was one of us, a vampire. And he was going to kill her.

She looked over her shoulder at him and yelped and began to run. He chased after her. I got out of the car and ran after them. I wasn't sure why, but I felt the need to see how this turned out. I didn't know if I could save her or not but I ran with the full intention of doing something. Maybe I ran out of curiosity. *How do other vamps do it?*

But before I could get close, I lost them. I ran around looking for them for a few minutes, then I heard her scream and raced into a back alley. I expected to see him draining her blood but he wasn't. He wasn't killing her. He was fucking her. And she was loving every minute of it. It was an old vampire-human game. The vamp does the chasing and the human does the running. Once the human's cornered, they're so hot they can't stand it. I'd heard of this game, even saw it played out a few times. Hugo and I never played it.

I tried to avert my eyes from the couple, but I couldn't. They were really into it, the way Hugo and I had always been into it with each other. She was panting and pressing up against him. A flash of Hugo and me raced though my mind and I almost passed out with that remembered passion. I watched them fucking—making love—and it made me so jealous I couldn't see straight. I don't know how long I stood there, but soon, I realized they weren't moving anymore.

"Oh, hello," she said and eyed me.

He turned and saw me and growled, "Do you mind?"

"Sorry," I said and started off.

"Don't go!" she yelled, then, "Charlie! Go get her!"

I ran quickly but he was suddenly in front of me. Old vampire trick. I did a disappearing act of my own but he came with me and I couldn't side-step the motherfucker for the life of me. I was about to try again when he grabbed my arm and pulled me into his chest. He was a lot stronger than I was. And a lot older.

Just then, she ran up to us, pushing the hair out of her face. As soon as he saw her, his face softened.

"You're one of them, aren't you?" she asked, all excited, then slapped Charlie on the chest. "I knew it! Didn't I tell you?"

I hissed at her. She glanced at him and then rolled her eyes.

"It's okay," he said. "I'm a vampire, too."

"I know that," I hissed. "Now let me go."

He let me go. I rubbed my wrists and glared at them.

"Why don't you stop by our pad?" she asked sweetly. "Charlie doesn't get to talk to many vamps."

I stared at them and shook my head. "No, I need to be going. It's getting light."

"Ah, come on," he said. "We can have a beer and swap stories."

"Yeah," she said. "Come on."

"It's okay," I said. "I'm sorry I interrupted you. I thought he was going to hurt you or something."

"Ah, that's okay," she said. "We were done by the time you got there. When we do this, I get so excited, I—"

"Cindy!" he half-yelled.

"Oops," she muttered. "Sorry."

I gave her a little smile and pointed over my shoulder with my thumb. "I'll just be going, then."

"No," she said and grabbed my hand. "Come with us. We won't hurt you or anything, will we Charlie?"

"What the hell could I do to her?" he asked. "She's dead."

"Don't say it like that," she said and shook her head at him. "He doesn't mean anything by it."

"It's okay," I said. "I know what I am."

"Well, come on," she said and linked her arm though mine, then stopped. "Oh, shit, the car's dead."

"Yeah, we broke down," Charlie said, looking around. "Then we lost track of time and... Uh, nevermind."

"We can take my car," I said quickly.

"We have to get a new car soon," Cindy told him. "That old piece of shit has to go."

"But I love that car," he said, almost whining.

She turned to me. "Why do some people get sentimental over things that don't work properly? That car has to go! It breaks down all the time!"

"Yeah, yeah," he said and turned to me. "So, you can drive us home?"

"Sure," I said. "Where do you live?"

"The suburbs," Cindy said.

"Oh," I muttered and they followed me to my car and we all got in. Charlie took the backseat and Cindy rode shotgun, giving me directions. I couldn't believe I was doing this but like I said, I had no fear since I became a vampire. It really did open me up. It's not so much that you can't trust people; it's more like if they did something to you, you know you could kill them. Or, in my case, you know they can't kill you.

As we drove, Cindy chatted up a storm. I smiled at her politely and wondered if she always talked so much.

"Yeah," Charlie said and chuckled. "She does."

I shook my head at him.

"Don't do that!" she yelled. "Did he read your mind?"

"Yeah," I said and closed it off.

"Sorry about that," she said and turned in her seat to glare at him. "He's so rude sometimes."

He chuckled again.

She swatted at him. "And don't do it to me, you bastard!"

He dodged her hand and laughed.

"He won't turn me," she said, turning back around.

"Why?" I asked.

"I dunno," she replied, then turned to him. "Why won't you turn me?"

"Let's don't start," he muttered.

"Yeah, let's do," she grumbled. "Why won't you just do it?"

"Because you know why," he grumbled back. "And we have a guest here so let's not get into it."

My stomach grumbled.

"Are you hungry?" she asked.

I nodded. "A little."

"We've got some blood," she said. "Unless you want to stop off for a kill."

I had to shake my head at her. "No, that's okay."

"You don't want to stop off?" she asked. "I know these horrendous drug dealers that really need it. They're totally turning this really nice neighborhood into a crack den."

"No," I said. "It's okay."

Charlie muttered something.

"What did you say?" she asked and turned to him.

"She doesn't kill," he said and then to me, "Do you?"

"Is it that obvious?" I asked.

"Yeah," he said. "It is."

"Oh, he doesn't kill, either," she said. "He was going to kill me but fell in love instead."

"Yeah," he said. "Love can really screw with being evil."

"How do you feed?" I asked and looked in the rear view mirror at him.

He said, "I have my sources."

I thought about that. What sort of sources? Maybe there was hope for me after all.

"It's not the same kind of taste," he said. "But it's okay. I just can't handle it anymore. The killing, I mean."

He almost acted as if he'd been a junkie before they met.

"I mean, I *can* kill," he said and stared at Cindy. "But I don't anymore."

"Oh, turn here," Cindy said and pointed.

I turned into a nice driveway of a very nice house.

"Like it?" she asked.

"Yeah," I said. "It's nice."

She nodded. "And worth it. It's got a full basement for him without any windows."

We got out and went inside. The house was spacious and furnished with taste. I'd always wanted a house like this, when I was human. Cindy settled me into a plush couch in the basement then went for "drinks", returning with two wine glasses full of blood.

"Thanks," I said and breathed it in, my mouth watering. I hadn't eaten in days.

"Drink all you want," she said and smiled. "We've got plenty."

"Thanks," I said again and took a sip. The blood coursed through my veins and made them pop to life. I shuddered with life and sucked it all down, then held my glass out to her.

"Must be hungry," she said and went for another glass.

"Where do you get the blood?" I asked Charlie.

"Blood bank," he said and nodded.

Why had I never thought of that? Well, I hadn't had to. Hugo had taken care of me, more or less, since he'd made me into a vampire. I had become overly dependent on him, I realized. Now I'd have to take care of myself. Knowing about the blood banks would definitely help.

"Hey, let me ask you something," he said. "How come you can't feed?"

I shrugged. "I don't know. I just can't."

"Not all of us kill, you know," he said. "I mean, we do, mostly, but we can turn it off and subsist on blood like that. We don't *have* to kill is what I'm trying to say."

I turned to him. "But you can kill if you want to, right?"

He nodded.

"What's it like?"

"What?"

"Killing."

He shrugged. "I dunno, its okay. I mean, it's...it's killing, taking someone's life so you can live."

"Do you miss it?"

He leaned forward and whispered, "Between you and me, yeah. But I never went after innocents, you know? Well, I did a few times. But that was a long time ago, when I first got turned."

"When you first got turned?"

"Yeah. You see, back then, there wasn't so much," he paused and used air quotes. "'Media attention' regarding us. Back then, it was easier to be what we are."

"Back then?" I asked, containing my eye roll. "What are you going to do? Tell me some sappy story of how you were made in the seventeenth century?"

"No," he said. "Actually, I was made in '72."

"1872?"

"1972," he said and nodded. "I was really stoned, too, and don't remember much of it."

Just then, Cindy came back into the room and said, "Hence the awful shag haircut."

She held out a fresh glass of blood to me. I smiled at her and took it gratefully, sucking about half down before she could blink.

She eyed me. "How long has it been since you ate?"

"A few days," I said.

"Damn," she muttered. "Want another?"

"No, thanks," I said.

"As I was saying," Charlie said and leaned forward. "They don't want to see us, the humans or whatever you want to call them. They pretend we're not real but we are."

She gave a little *ahem* sound.

"Oh, I mean most of them," he continued. "They don't want to explain all the unexplained deaths and disappearances that happen in this country."

It was so dark, so gory.

"And they're scared shitless," he said. "Making up little stories about good and bad vampires. Truth is, we're neither good nor bad. We're a mixture of the two. Just like them except it's a lot easier for us to kill."

I nodded, wondering why he was telling me all this. It was like he was a stoner who was high out of his mind and had sudden clarity that only he could understand.

"We are misfits of society," he said. "Not recognized but certainly not welcomed."

As soon as the words were out of his mouth, a really tall, beautiful blonde walked into the room. She stopped and stared at me. I stared back and at once knew she was like me.

"Who's she?" she asked.

"This is Lola," Cindy said. "Now be nice."

She and I eyed each other, then she held out her hand and said, "I'm Marcella."

"Marcella?" I asked before I could stop myself.

"Would I lie about a name like Marcella?" she scoffed and sat down on the couch near me, lighting a cigarette. "He made you, didn't he? Hugo, I mean."

I turned my head to her but didn't answer. How did she know that?

"I can tell his work a mile away," she said, smoking. "Where is the old bastard?"

I still didn't answer.

"Ah!" she exclaimed and pointed at me. "He left you! He was always a heartbreaker."

I turned on her. "What do you know about it?"

"Apparently more than you," she said.

"Shut up, Marcella!" Cindy snapped. "You don't know shit and you just met Lola!"

"Fuck off, cunt!" Marcella snapped back.

"Bitch!" Cindy shouted and jumped to her feet.

Marcella was on her in a second and they were circling each other, as if a catfight was about to ensue.

"Girls!" Charlie yelled and stepped between them, pushing them apart. "None of that tonight."

"You've got to get rid of her, Charlie!" she yelled. "I can't stand this anymore! I'm going to stake her!"

"Like hell," she said. "I'll drain every ounce of blood out of your skinny ass! I mean, if I could even stand to touch you, which I can't!"

"Mom, come on," Charlie said.

I almost fell off the couch. "Did you just call her mom?"

He turned to me. "Well, she *is* my mom."

I just stared at him.

"Yeah, he turned *her* but he won't turn *me*," Cindy seethed. "Son of a bitch."

"Watch your mouth!" Marcella snapped.

"Wait a minute," I said to Charlie. "You turned your mother?"

He nodded. "She was really sick. I didn't realize she'd go back to her youth or anything. It does that, you know?" Then he turned to Cindy. "And I turned her years and years ago, Cindy, way before we met. So, none of this."

I almost smiled.

Cindy huffed and stomped out of the room. Charlie sighed loudly and went after her. Marcella turned to me and offered me her pack of cigarettes. I took one, she lit it and I inhaled.

"Thanks," I said. "How do you know about Hugo?"

"Oh, honey, that was years ago, just after Charlie turned me," she said, smiling in memory. "I was like a wild child, sowing my wild oats."

"Were you two lovers?" I asked, feeling slightly jealous.

"Yeah," she said nonchalantly. "But we weren't in love. Back then, I was just in love with being a vamp, feeling alive for the first time."

I nodded. I knew how she felt.

"Hugo used to turn a lot of young girls like you," she said. "Young, beautiful, and sad."

"Excuse me?"

"Damaged," she said. "He was always trying to save someone."

I looked away.

"He has an affection for the lost souls of the world," she said. "Probably because he was so lost himself."

I nodded.

"He told me he'd been turned so young he couldn't ever remember being young," she said.

"I know," I said. "He told me the same thing."

She nodded. "The one who turned him killed herself."

I knew this.

She went on nonetheless, "That's why he wants to save so many."

"How did she kill herself?" I asked.

"By sitting in the sun," she said and gave a wry smile.

"Why do you think she did it?" I asked.

"Because she got tired of living," she replied.

"Oh," I muttered.

"We're cursed," she said. "It is a curse but somehow a blessing in disguise. Just like love."

And that's what it was exactly. A curse, but a blessing in disguise. We bleed others dry, we steal their lives so we could live but at the same time, we are dead.

"Go to the witch," she said out of nowhere.

"Excuse me?" I asked.

"The witch," she said. "You've heard of her, haven't you?"

I shook my head.

"If you want him back, and I can tell you do," she said. "Go to the witch. She'll help you and if she can't, no one can."

As soon as the words were out of her mouth, a tall, gangly guy walked in. When he saw us, he stopped short then said, "Oh, hello."

"Hi, baby," she said and smiled at him. "This is Lola."

"Hi, Lola," he said. "I'm Tom."

He was something else besides a Tom. He wasn't human but he wasn't a vamp, I could just tell. Being a vampire, it was easy to pick up on when someone wasn't human. It's the smell; they had a very different smell. I had to ask, "What are you?"

"Werewolf," he said.

"Oh," I said, thinking I'd never met a werewolf before.

"So, Lola, what are you in town for?"

"Actually, I was just leaving," I said and stood.

"She's going to see the witch," Marcella told him.

"Oh, good," he said. "It's always good to see the witch."

"I don't think I'm going to her, actually," I said, edging closer to the door.

"Oh, go see her," he said. "You'll be glad you did. Go see the witch."

I went to the witch.

Empty Promises.

I always felt alone in the world, even when I was married, even though I belonged to a big family. I always felt left out, overlooked, unwanted. Hugo was the only person who ever made me feel right with myself. And I had let him down. I couldn't be what he wanted and needed me to be—a bloodsucking killer. I thought about that now and then I remembered the young couple he'd brought home for our dinner years ago.

"Feed!" Hugo roared.

I stared at the young couple, but not into their eyes. I looked away quickly, not able to see what I was seeing—the fear. They'd been mesmerized. Now they were full of it, full of fear. I could feel their fear. It was so strong I almost gagged. I sent him a message: *Please don't make me do this, Hugo.* He ignored me, as he always did during times like this. He was going to make me do it, even if killed me—or them, the young attractive couple. The couple who didn't know what they were getting into when he lied to them and told them he had some good drugs in his apartment. All they had to do was follow him home and he'd let them have all they wanted. I looked away from it all and wished I'd never seen Hugo. But then I felt bad for that thought and wished he'd never turned me. Then I thought, *When are the drugs going to start working on them?* They'd consumed so much, they should be out of their minds. But they were alert, attentive, and scared shitless. Kinda like I was.

"FEED!" he roared again and grabbed my arm and shoved me over to them. "Now. Do it!"

I grabbed her arm and sank my teeth down into it. The first trickle of blood made me gag and, before I knew what I was doing, I was up and running towards the bathroom. He caught me in the hallway, grabbed my arm and threw me up against the wall.

"What the fuck is wrong with you?" he spat. "Tell me where I went wrong."

"I just can't do it," I cried. "Let me go."

There was a rustle in the living room. They were trying to escape. We stared towards the doorway and then he was gone, chasing them. I sank to the floor and began to cry. I don't know how long I was there but suddenly he was standing over me. I jumped and he thrust his arm out to me. I stared up at him and he nodded. I grabbed his arm and began to feed off of him. He let me feed for a good five minutes, then pushed me away.

"Why can't you do it?" he asked softly.

"I—I just can't," I said. "I don't know why, but I just can't."

He stared at me. "Lola, you have to start doing this soon. We can't keep this up."

I nodded. "I'll do better next time."

"I saved the girl for last," he said and walked away.

I wanted to call after him, *Don't!* But I couldn't. I had drained him and now he would drain her.

"Are you coming?!" he roared.

No, I wasn't. I sat there and put my hands over my ears as I heard her screams, then her submission. Then it was quiet again. I looked up and saw him coming towards me. I stood up and waited until he pressed his mouth against mine. I opened my mouth and he pushed the pretty young girl's blood from his mouth into mine. I took it all. He stepped back from me, then he went into the living room. Then he came back and gave me some more blood. He did this again and again until she was completely drained.

Afterwards, I promised to do better next time. And the next time, I promised to do the same thing. Again and again I promised something I had no way of keeping. I guess Hugo finally got fed up with me and my empty promises.

I felt my heart turn cold again towards him. He didn't have to torture people the way he did. He could do it more gently, more quickly. He could make it easier on them. But he didn't because he was a vampire and he wanted me to be exactly like him. He wanted me whole or nothing. No half-vamps for him. He wanted a killer who relished the kill. To him I wasn't worthy.

And then he started to get mean. He was so disappointed in me, he refused to feed me. I'd lie for days, sometimes for weeks, without anything to eat. He'd tell me if I got hungry enough I'd do it. But he was wrong. I'd never be that hungry. I couldn't do it. I couldn't take life, not like him.

"That's life, Lola," he said after once such incident. "You're born and then you live and then you die. It's the way of life."

I looked away from him. I was so hungry, my stomach lurched. I rose up out of bed and cried out. Then I began to beg, "Please, Hugo, feed me."

"You have to do it, Lola."

"I can't!" I wailed. "Please, please, please! For God's sake, feed me!"

He shook his head and leaned back against the wall.

I stared at him and mustered the courage to get out of bed. I fell to the floor and crawled over to him. He watched me with dispassion. When I got to him, I grabbed onto his legs and pulled myself up. I mumbled, "Please."

"Do it yourself."

"No!" I screamed. "Feed me! You can't just do this to me and leave me without anything! You can't starve me to death!"

"You won't starve to death," he said. "Stop being so melodramatic."

"Hugo, please," I said and started to cry. "Please."

"No," he snapped. "Now stop asking me."

Then I got so pissed off, I found some strength. I pulled myself up and stared him dead in the eye. He stared back as if he were wondering what I was going to do. I punched him right across the mouth. Before I could blink, he backhanded me and I went sailing across the room. I landed against the wall with a thump. I looked up to see the indentation my body had made in the wall, then turned back to him. Oh, no, he was coming for me.

He stomped over to me, pulled me up like I was a rag doll and hissed, "Don't ever hit me again!"

I found more strength and slapped him. His head shot to the side and his eyes darkened. He threw me to the side and stomped out of the room. I screamed, "Come back here!"

I heard the front door slam and he was gone. For a whole week. I lay on the floor, unable to move, for a whole week. I was in and out of consciousness. Then, I felt his presence and then I felt his arms around me, picking me up and putting me to bed. And then, finally, relief as he pushed a glass at my mouth. I grabbed it hungrily and sucked the blood down. After I was done, I asked for another. He got me another glass, then another. In a matter of minutes, I was alive again. I stared at him and noticed he was watching me incredulously. His face was hard and I wondered if he despised me as much as his look said he did.

"I'm sorry," he said.

"Me too," I told him.

He turned to me and his face softened. He was sorry that he couldn't make me into something I was incapable of being. He smoothed the hair back from my face and said softly, "When I was younger, I always wondered why I did it; how I could do it, kill someone like that. But as I grew older, I understood that if not me, something else."

I shook my head. I didn't want him to explain it to me. I didn't want to understand any of it. Nevertheless, he went on.

"If I don't do it, Lola," he said. "Something else will. They're just going to die anyway eventually, so why not kill them? This way, it's quick and easy and somewhat humane."

"You're disgusting."

"You eat them, too," he said. "So what does that make you?"

"Shut up."

"Listen," he said. "Without them, you can't survive. Accept, Lola, accept what you are now."

"I can't," I muttered.

"You can," he said. "You can do it. I know you can."

But I couldn't. I couldn't rationalize it in my mind. I dropped my head and muttered, "It's not right, Hugo."

"What is right, Lola, or for that matter, wrong?" he asked softly and pushed the hair back from my eyes again. "This is what we are, what we were made to do and you have to accept that. Right or wrong, good or bad, we are killers. I didn't ask to be turned, I just was. I had to find my way and I had to survive. That's all it's about, survival. The strongest survive. And we are strong. You have to accept that you are strong now."

But I didn't feel strong, I felt weak, inconsequential. I felt all the things he abhorred. I hated myself for not being able to do what I needed to do in order to survive. I hated that he had to feed me.

"Out hearts don't beat and we don't breathe," he said. "The only way we can survive is to take someone's breath. Learn to live with that."

But I couldn't.

★ ★ ★ ★ ★

On my way out of Cleveland, I drove around and found a blood bank. As it was still early in the morning, I was able to break in and steal some blood. The alarm went off but I ignored it, knowing I'd be out of there before anyone showed up. I grabbed several packs of blood and put them in a little cooler I'd purchased at a convenience store. That would do me for days. Once I opened the package and began to drain it, I felt a surge of power soar through my veins. I felt myself grow warm for an instant, the way he always made me feel.

"My love," he had whispered once. "Show me how much you love me. Get down on your knees and show me."

I got down on my knees and stared up at him, rubbing him through his pants. He was hard and wanting me. I unzipped his pants and took his member in my mouth, sucking gently on it until he moaned.

I didn't have time to do much more. He grabbed me up under the arms and threw me across the bed and fell on top of me. Then he began to ravage my body, taking his time to kiss and caresses me before he began to undress me. And once I was naked, completely and totally naked under his hungry eye, he fell down on top of me and took me. He took me without a single word; he took me knowing that's what I wanted. I wanted him to take me, to bring me under his control. That way, I couldn't back away from what was about to happen.

We began to move together, in sync. We stared into each other's eyes as we moved, as we made love, as we fucked. Our stares didn't waver an inch. We were fucking and we knew we were fucking. There was no shame in it. It was what we were made to do and do it we did. We did it hard and fast and furious, as if we couldn't get enough. And truth be told, we couldn't.

All of a sudden, I was soaring above myself as the orgasm exploded inside of me, as if it were dying to get out. I grabbed onto him and held on for dear life. He was so close to me then, so close it was as if we were one person. And, maybe we were.

"Oh, Lola," he moaned as he came. "I love you so fucking much!"

Yeah, right, I thought as I drove away from the blood bank. He loved me, loved me, loved me. Loved me so much he'd leave me hanging, waiting. Dying a slow horrible death but not dying at all, leaving me forever in a state of hunger, hanging onto life by a sheer thread. The hunger was unending. It was terrible and made me cry out in pain. There was no relief from the hunger, not even death. All I could do was hang on and wait. And he'd make me wait, sometimes for days and weeks. He'd make me wait just to make me suffer.

"But I do," he said once. "I do love you."

"Crock of shit," I muttered, fuming. He didn't love me. If he loved me, he wouldn't have left me. I glanced over at the cooler and smiled smugly to myself. Thank God I'd met Charlie. I knew how to feed myself now. I didn't need Hugo anymore. But he was going to pay for leaving me like that, leaving me to shrivel. I had my blood and I didn't need him.

Now I could go see the witch.

The witch.

The witch lived in Charleston, South Carolina. I was about two weeks into my hunt when I finally made it there. I drove all night and slept all day with the curtains drawn on the cheap motel windows.

The witch wasn't at all pleased to see me. Not that I cared. As I stared at her tiny frame and long hair, I thought she looked less like a witch than a Stevie Nicks wannabe. Her gypsy type outfit consisted of a long skirt and peasant blouse which hung loosely on her thin body. Her steely blue eyes stared right through me. She wouldn't let me into her house.

"You're not coming in here," she said.

"I'm not here to hurt you," I told her. "I just want a spell."

"You couldn't hurt me if you wanted to," she snapped. "And what kind of spell do you want?"

"I need to find someone."

She leaned back and eyed me. "I've heard about you. You're the one who can't kill."

I sighed with annoyance. Did everyone in the world know about me and my condition? Yes, I suppose they did. I was gossip—the vampire who couldn't kill.

"Please," I said, preparing myself to beg. I hated to do that. I hated to show weakness, to ask for favors, or for that matter, sympathy. But I'd do it to get her to help me.

She eyed me, then shook her head with annoyance and said, "Okay, you can come in but if you try anything, you'll be sorry."

I resisted the urge to smirk and walked into her overly decorated house. It was filled with pink flowers and pink furniture and was just so...*pink*. It looked like a big bottle of pepto bismo had exploded inside the room.

"Nice place," I said dryly. "By the way, I'm Lola."

"Stop being polite," she said and sat on the couch. "Just sit down and tell me what you want so I can tell you I can't help you."

"I'm looking for someone," I said. "Hugo, he's a vampire."

"I've heard of him," she said. "He's the one who turned you, I suppose?"

I nodded.

"He was here not too long ago," she said.

"Really?" I asked but stopped myself from sounding too excited. With as much nonchalance as I could muster, I said, "What did he want?"

She eyed me warily and said, "None of your business."

I had a sudden urge to kill her. I couldn't, of course, but I had an urge.

"Oh, forget it," she said, sounding almost sympathetic. "He wanted a spell, that's all."

"What kind of spell?" I had to ask.

"Nothing fancy," she said. "Just some sort of cure thing."

"Cure?" I asked. "Cure for what?"

She eyed me. "I'm not sure but I couldn't help him. He was very disappointed that I couldn't but I can't help everyone and I especially don't like to help vampires. So he left with no more than he came."

"Oh," I said and let it go. Was he sick? Was there something wrong with him? What did he want with a cure? And what was the cure for? I stared at her. She'd never give it up, not even if I tortured her. So I gave up the urge to ask her for any more information. Besides that wasn't what I was here for.

"How long were you with him?" she asked.

"About ten years."

"And during this time you couldn't kill?"

I shook my head. "No. I tried to, of course, but I couldn't. It would make me sick."

"As it should," she said dryly. "It's my opinion that all of you should die. But you don't though. You just keep repopulating yourselves, like rabbits or vermin."

I let her little dig slide and asked, for some reason, "Why do you think I can't kill?"

She eyed me before replying, "Well, that's easy. You can't kill because you really don't want to. You know, deep down, that it's wrong."

"But all vamps want to kill."

"Not all, not really," she said. "Not all kill and mostly those who don't don't because they're lazy or have some other reason. Perhaps Hugo left you because of this reason. He wanted you to be more like him and when you couldn't, he couldn't take it. Maybe you made him feel guilt over what he was doing. After all, it *is* evil."

"Tell me something I don't know," I muttered.

"But you're different," she said. "You don't kill because you can't and that's what sets you apart from the rest."

I stared at her, knowing she was right but wishing she was wrong.

"Enough of the bullshit," she said. "Tell me what you want."

"Answers," I said.

"And what are the questions?"

I paused before I said, "Why did he stop loving me?"

"Who says he did?"

My head jerked up. I hadn't thought about it like that. Maybe he still loved me. Maybe I was just fooling myself. How could he love me if he left me?

"You're obsessed," she said, very matter-of-factly. "You're obsessed with him, with what he's doing. You want to know whether or not he has his arms wrapped around another woman."

I blanched. Yeah. I was obsessed, especially with the other woman thing. I had visions of him taking another woman, turning her into one of us and of them running around the world together, as we had run. I had hatred for that woman, for her stepping into my shoes, for taking over my rightful place.

"I don't understand you vampires," she said and lit a stick of incense. "You're soulless creatures, you take the lives of others but at the same time you love like you're still human."

I nodded but looked away. She was right. We did love with wild abandon. We loved so fiercely and so loyally that we suffocated each other. Had I suffocated him? Was that why he left me?

"Love is a funny thing," she said. "Just when you give up on it, you get it and when you get it, you can't live without it and then that's when it usually goes away. Is that the way you feel, Lola?"

I shrugged. The incense was making my stomach churn. It always did. I hated it, always had. I had a sudden urge to run from the room.

"It is the way you feel, isn't it?" she said, smiling slightly. "You gave it away and now you're empty without it."

I wished she'd shut up.

"And you gave it all away for this love, for Hugo," she said. "The thing you don't understand is that we don't really love others. We love how they make us feel. They awaken us and with them, we begin to love ourselves. Once they take that love away, we feel hatred for ourselves and we begin to blame, blame them for leaving us when, in fact, it's our insecurity that's at play and torturing us."

I rolled my eyes. She was so full of shit. She wasn't a witch. She was a psuedo-psychologist.

"This is why we always want more," she continued, really getting into goading me. "Seeking the one who will fulfill us indefinitely. Or so we think."

I turned back to her and said, "I suppose now you're just going to tell me to love myself and just forget about it."

"No," she said. "You can't do that. You have to have others to bring it out in you. Otherwise, it lays dormant and you find yourself alone crying for someone, something to make you love yourself. You want to give yourself but have no one to give yourself to."

"Whatever," I said. "Are you help me with the spell or not?"

"You don't need a spell," she said quickly.

"But that's what I'm here for."

"Forget about the spell for now, Lola," she said. "And concentrate on why you're running after this vampire."

"Because I'm going to kill him," I said.

She threw her head back and laughed. "You're going to kill him? Oh, that's rich."

"I am," I said with indignation. "I am going to kill him."

"Why?" she asked, still laughing.

"Well, because I'll go back to being human then, won't I?"

She stared at me. "I don't know if that works or not. I've never seen any evidence of it. But then again, it wouldn't hurt to kill him and find out. It would be one less vampire in the world and that's always a good thing. So go ahead and give it a try. I wouldn't get my hopes up, though."

"I'm going to do it," I said.

"Yeah, okay," she said. "Why are you really going to kill him? Because he left you?"

"Well, yeah," I said. "And he's done a lot of killing himself. He deserves to die and I'm the one who's going to make sure he does."

"Don't fool yourself," she said. "You are not on a journey of vengeance. You are on a journey to find the one who finally woke you up inside."

"No," I said evenly. "I want to kill him."

"Perhaps," she said. "But you also want him to love you."

I sighed.

"Through others," she said. "Through their eyes, we see ourselves, don't we? We see how we really are, how we really act, how good we can become. We see ourselves standing in time, being what we always wanted to be. That is what we crave."

"Whatever," I said, getting annoyed. The incense was becoming too much but I knew if I put it out, she'd get pissed.

"Don't 'whatever' me," she snapped. "I hate the 'whatever'. It's so childish."

I rolled my eyes and said, "Can you do a spell or not?"

"What sort of spell do you want?" she asked and lit another incense stick.

I forced myself not to put the incense out and said, "I just want a spell to help find him, that's all."

"What good would that do?" she asked, shaking out the match. "By the time you found him, he'd be gone."

"Well, can't you do something that would track him?"

"I could do that, yeah, you could track him," she said softly. "But he'd be gone by the time you got there."

"I'm pretty quick."

"You're not that quick," she told me.

"So do a spell and let's find out." I was getting agitated and it showed. "If you don't help me, I'll hurt you. I might not kill you, but I can hurt you. I'm *very* strong."

"You can't hurt me," she said dismissively. "Before you lifted a hand to me, I'd have your teeth knocked down your damn throat. And what good is a toothless vampire?"

She gave a good cackle at her wry remark. I groaned. She was such a bitch.

"Would you like me to demonstrate?" she asked as if she couldn't wait to try.

"No, but I can hurt you," I said and grabbed a big crystal from the coffee table and started to throw it at her. "Now do it."

She tutted me, shaking her head. "Put the crystal down. That thing cost a fortune."

"Please," I said, shaking the crystal. "Help me."

She raised her hand and the crystal disappeared from my hand and into hers. That really pissed me off. She set it gently back down on the coffee table before saying, "He's headed south, Lola, deeper south."

"Obviously, I know that," I said. "But where?"

"You know where," she said and stood. "Now it's time for you to leave. I have some work to do."

"You're a bitch," I said.

"And you're pathetic," she shot back. "Chasing after a man who doesn't want to be found. What are you going to say to him when you catch up, Lola?"

"I guess I'll just ask how he's doing," I said dryly.

"Sometimes, it's best to leave well enough alone," she said. "In most cases it is. Figure it out and move on with your own life instead of chasing someone who obviously doesn't want you."

I cringed.

"He has his reasons," she said. "So let it be."

"I can't," I said.

"Then go," she said. "Go south and find him and beg him for answers that you know in your heart already."

I stared at her and started to say something about her being a lying bitch when she suddenly disappeared. *Fuck!* I stood and kicked the coffee table; it flew across the room. Then I sat back down in a huff and crossed my arms.

What a waste of time this had been. Even though she'd told me what I needed to hear, I couldn't comprehend it. And I couldn't comprehend it because I didn't want to, not just yet, maybe not ever. Not ever was a long damn time to be stubborn about something.

A woman scorned.

The chase continued but it was becoming harder and harder to keep up with him. He became an obsession to me. He became the hunted, but was I really hunting myself? Had the witch been right? Was this all about my insecurity, my inability to face up to the truth? Was I deluding myself into believing in something that might not have been there from the beginning? I didn't know and at that point, I didn't really care. All I knew was that I had to find him.

I chased him through most of the South. Through the Carolinas and then down to Florida, even to Miami. I was sure he'd go on to Key West just to piss me off because it was always so hot and sunny there. But then his direction changed and I lost him, once again.

This began to get really old.

I kept on, as only a woman scorned can. I kept the chase up, hot on his heels, just missing him everywhere I went.

But I didn't even think about giving up. Giving up wasn't in my blood or in my ability when it came to Hugo. I was going to finish this one way or another.

As I chased, as I drove that old, worn-out car, crisscrossing the South, I would think of us, how we'd been together, how we'd loved. I would think about the good times, the happy times, then I'd think about the sex, the hot intensity of it, its animalistic nature. There were many things I remembered—the coolness of his skin as I pressed myself against him, the sharpness of his teeth as he nibbled on my nipple, the power of his eyes as he took me.

After a kill, he'd be especially ready to give me all he had. He would push himself deep down into me. He would savor me, take me. He could do anything and everything he wanted to do to me and I would beg for it. He would tie me up, he would take me down. I went willingly, all for the sex, all for the pleasure.

And now missing that pleasure in my life was tormenting me. I still wanted him, still needed him. Why did I have to need him like that? He was so strong and I relied on his strength much more than I'd allowed myself to believe. He was stronger than me, even when I drained him of all his power.

There was one time when I'd almost taken all the blood he had. I'd sucked so hard on his arm, loving the feeling of his blood mingling with mine, that I had to have it. I couldn't stop. He had to throw me away from him but I went right back in, trying to get the blood, trying to drain every ounce from him and put it into me.

"Get off!" he hissed and pushed me away.

"Give it to me!" I screamed once and tried to hit him.

He dodged me and shook his head. "Try it, Lola, and see me tear you from limb to limb."

Maybe that's what I couldn't stand, the thought that he was so much stronger than me. Maybe I thought I could take his power if I drained him of all his blood. Maybe I thought I could somehow be more like him if I had it all. *Give it to me! Give me the blood! Make me whole!*

I tried again. He pushed me away from him, more gently than before, and shook his head at me.

"That's your last warning, Lola."

"Then don't do this to me," I cried. "Don't do this!"

"Do what?" he asked softly and walked over to me.

"Bring those people in here and suck them dry," I said. "Don't bring them here. Do it somewhere else. I can't stand their smell!"

He chuckled and shook his head at me, which infuriated me even more.

"I can't do this," I said. "I just can't. Please don't bring anyone else into our house again."

"You'll get weak," he said, bending down to stare into my eyes. "*Weak.* Slowly you'll shrivel and become skin and bones but you won't die. You'll just be a husk. All your beauty will be lost. Is that what you want, Lola?"

"You know it isn't," I hissed and before I could stop myself, I had slapped him across the mouth.

His head shot to the side and his lip bled. Then he turned on me and his eyes seemed to light up. I was almost frightened, almost scared and started to back away from him. I didn't get the chance. He threw me across the room. I fell with a thud and became infuriated. I got right back up and was at him. We attacked each other, each trying to bring the other down. And he won, as he always did. I succumbed and began to lick and kiss at his mouth, which was stained red from the blood he'd just consumed.

"Give it to me," I moaned and grabbed onto his cock. "Give it all to me, baby. Now!"

"Like this?" he asked and began to push me up against the wall.

"Oh, yeah," I said as he grabbed my breasts. "Fuck me."

I didn't have to tell him twice. He had the clothes, literally, ripped from my body in an instant and he was filling me up, consuming me. I loved to be consumed by him, to take it all, to give it back. We were alone then, as we always were. Our foreheads pressed up against the others and our eyes never wavered for a second. He was taking me and I liked being taken.

He drove it in harder and I gasped from the pain, from the pleasure. He was the best I'd ever had and he had it all—he had the looks and the intensity and the "don't mess with me" attitude, which made me want to mess with him even more, of course. He set the fire in my heart and he stoked it, just like he was stoking me, as he was taking me. It was too much and I was too turned on and before I could stop myself, I threw my head back and moaned loudly with the orgasm as it swept though my body, as it gave me peace and understanding. And what I understood was simple. He had my heart. He had all of me, probably always would.

I didn't mind that one bit.

* * * * *

We try all our lives to forget about the past, about the things that hurt us. Hugo made me forget but he brought new pain into my life. Pain that I relished, but also pain that almost killed me. Pain I wish I could forget.

"Take it," he had said.

I looked up at him, standing there beside the bed. It was an effort to look up because I was so weak. He had taken to not feeding me for days and I would lie and stare at the ceiling being trapped in an endless purgatory of hunger. I would lay there and pray for his return, for the blood.

"Take it," he said again and shoved a glass of blood at me.

I tried to restrain myself and not be greedy, but I couldn't help it. The hunger took over. I grabbed at the glass and gulped it down. It was cold, as if it had been in the refrigerator for hours. I didn't care. It was blood, nourishment, what I needed. I didn't look up until the glass was empty.

He grunted. I looked away in embarrassment but now, with this stranger's blood in my system, I felt alive and ready.

I reached out for him and he let me take his hand. I pulled him down on the bed and began to kiss him, greedily kiss him until he moaned and settled on top of me, ready to give me his body. That day we made love and it was soundless. It was quiet but no less intense than it had been.

He took me over, pushing my arms above my head and running his hands down the insides of my arms until he got to my breasts which he stroked softly, then with more vigor, more pressure, until my nipples were raised hard and alert. His mouth was on them then, on my nipples, going to and fro until each had been adequately covered. I moaned with each touch, each suck and each lip, ready as ever for him to take me and make me whole.

And then he did. He took me. He just took me over, ramming into me, making me cry out for his mercy. But I didn't want him to stop; I wanted what he wanted and I wanted him to fuck me silly, to take me over the edge, to give it to me. It was selfish that I wanted his passion, even if it did come wrapped in his wrath. I wanted it as much as he wanted to give it to me. And I took it because it made me feel alive. It made me feel needed but most importantly it made me feel wanted.

"Ahh!" I cried out as my hips rose off the bed, as the orgasm came at me and made me whole.

He kept at it until we were both spent and panting. Then he moved off me, lay beside me and stared at the ceiling. That's when I knew it had changed, something had changed and there wasn't a damn thing I could do about it. Just as there wasn't a thing I could do about him rising from the bed and heading to the door.

"Get some rest," he said and left the room.

I closed my eyes and when I awoke the next day, everything in our relationship seemed to shift. I foolishly thought we were beginning a new era, even though a little voice in my head told it was the beginning of the end. Hugo told me I was going to start going out with him. He said he was going to make me help him with the victims. We'd go to supermarkets late at nights and to clubs and to bars. We'd find our prey and then we'd eat them.

And that's what we did. For a year, we went out every night and I had a hand in every victim's demise. I fed well during that year but I never once killed.

On that last night, I realized he had done that to show me how it was done. He had taught me well and then he'd left me to my own devices. And now I was ready to really find him. I was ready to get this done so I could move on with my life in which ever direction it was going to go.

I sat down on the motel room floor and closed my eyes. I was going to find him myself. If that bitch the witch wouldn't help me, I'd do it. I'd bought some spell books and some herbs. I had everything I needed. I lit the candles and then the stage was set. It was time to stop messing around and find him once and for all.

I began to hum and to chant the spell over and over: *Wherever you walk, wherever you wallow, stop right now and let me follow... Wherever you walk, wherever you wallow, stop right now and let me follow... Wherever you walk, wherever you wallow, stop right now and let me follow...*

All of a sudden, I felt myself become lighter than air and I might have levitated, if I'd opened my eyes to see, but I couldn't open my eyes, lest I break the spell. That I didn't want. I wanted this done and I put every ounce of energy I had into it.

Then I saw him. I had brought him to me, just like the witch refused to teach me to do. I almost cried when I saw him. He was walking along a crowed street. I sensed a familiarity but I couldn't figure out where he was. But there he was, somewhere out there in the world and he was walking quickly, with purpose.

I smiled. I couldn't help myself. I felt all the love I had for him devour me and beg for him to look at me and reciprocate. *Hugo, come to me! Hugo, you know I'm here. Turn around and talk to me, tell me why. I have to know why.*

He picked up his pace and disappeared for a moment. I thought I had lost him but then there he was again, turning around in a vaguely familiar old hotel room. He turned around and then sat at the edge of the bed, on top of the ragged chenille blanket. A flicker of recognition blinked in my mind at the blanket but was gone almost immediately. I turned to him.

Hugo, I'm waiting.

He crossed his arms and said, "Lola, please stop this."

He knew I was watching him! I was there with him even though we were miles apart! But wait a minute, he wasn't happy to see me. But then again, I hadn't expected that he would be, even though I had hoped he'd somehow want to see me, even if I was just a vision in his room.

"Lola," he said more seriously. "Please stop this."

"Hugo," I said. "Please give me one minute."

"Why are you doing this? How are you doing this?" he asked, then nodded slowly. "Oh."

"What is it?" I asked.

He smiled. "I see you've visited our little friend, the witch. I should have killed her when I had the chance."

"You couldn't have," I said. "She can disappear at whim."

"Oh, yeah," he muttered. "Please leave me alone."

"No," I said. "I am not going to do that, not after all we've been through."

"And what have we been through that makes what we had so special?" he asked and stood from the bed. "Get over this and leave me alone. Don't come to me like this ever again or one night you'll find me standing beside you bed and, believe me, you won't be happy to see me."

"But Hugo, I need to see you," I said. "I need to see you because—"

"I know why," he said. "I know what you plan to do. It's written all over your face."

My shoulders slumped.

"If that's what you want to do," he said. "I can't stop you."

I started to say something, but then stopped.

"You know where I am," he said and walked away and out of the vision.

My eyes popped open. Just then, it occurred to me. He was in New Orleans.

Scene of the original crime.

How very typical of Hugo to go back to our old stomping ground of New Orleans. How very typical of him to go back to the scene of the original crime, to the place where we'd met. How very typical of him to "allow" me to find him in the very hotel room where he'd made me, sitting on the bed where I'd changed forever. That's where he was and that's where I would find him.

Of course, by the time I got there, he wouldn't be in the hotel room any longer. So, I walked around the Quarter all night looking for him in the bars he liked to frequent. I caught his scent at a really old Irish pub and was about to walk out when I noticed this guy staring at me. I stared back and we nodded. He was one of us. He was a vamp. But I didn't have time for him.

I began to walk quickly, trying to get out of the bar before he came over. I did not want to stop for a chat. All vampires think that all other vampires always want to talk to them, like we were all members of the same club or something. I didn't. Not today, not tonight. I was on a mission.

I got out of the bar and walked up the street. But then there he was, at my side, grinning. He was tall and dark, of course, and fairly good looking. He had a rather large nose which looked like it'd just been broken and hadn't healed yet.

"I'm Lawrence," he said and held out his hand.

I stopped and said, "Lawrence, I don't have time for this. I'm looking for someone."

"Hugo, right?" he asked.

"How did you know?"

"You're Lola," he said. "Everyone knows about you and Hugo."

My interest was piqued, but I still didn't have time for this. I told him, "I don't have time for this."

"Come sit with me," he said. "Hugo's not going anywhere."

"Why?" I asked.

"Don't you want to talk?"

"Yeah," I said. "I do. To Hugo."

"In time," he said and motioned me into a bar. "Come with me."

I shrugged. This vamp wasn't going to take no for an answer. "One beer, then I have to leave," I said and followed him in. Maybe this guy knew Hugo, maybe he could help me. Probably all he wanted to do was sit around and bullshit, as most vamps did.

He got us two beers and brought them to the little booth I was sitting at. "Here."

"Thanks," I said and picked it up. "One beer, then I have to leave."

He nodded. "I know. You said that already."

I sighed and said, "So what's this about?"

He smiled and sipped his beer but didn't say anything. He was really beginning to irritate me.

I said again, "So what's this about?"

"I just wanted to meet you," he said and pulled a pack of cigarettes out, lighting two.

I took the cigarette, inhaled and asked, "Why did you want to meet me?"

"You're famous," he said.

"Excuse me?"

"You're the vamp who can't kill," he said. "Everyone knows about you. If it wasn't for Hugo protecting you, you'd know how famous you are. But he's kept you hidden. At least until recently."

"But I thought there were others like me," I said.

He shook his head. "Who told you that? You're the only one."

"I'm the only one?" I asked, even though I pretty much realized that.

"Yeah, you are," he said, smoking.

"But why would Hugo keep me, as you said, hidden?"

"Probably didn't want anyone to know that you're the one," he said.

"The one?"

He stared at me. "You have no idea, do you?"

"About what?"

He sighed. "Damn. You really don't know, do you?"

"About what?" I asked, feeling panicky maybe this guy did know something I didn't.

"But it's really you, right? You're Lola?"

"Yes, I am," I said. "Now tell me what you mean."

"Hmm," he said. "It's so odd to be sitting here with you."

"What's so odd about it?"

"It's just odd," he said. "It's just so odd."

"Get on with it," I said. "Tell me what you mean."

He shrugged.

"And besides, it's not my fault I can't do it," I said.

"No, it's not," he said. "It's a curse, that's all."

"A curse?"

He nodded. "Yeah, everyone knows."

"I didn't."

"That's because he's protected you," he said. "For what? Five years?"

I nodded. "Ten years. But anyway, forget all this other bullshit because it won't matter much longer. I'm going to kill Hugo."

He laughed, rather harshly, at my naiveté. "Sure, you are."

"Fuck you," I growled.

"Listen, everyone knows," he said.

"And what do they know?" I spat.

"Hugo turned you into a killer who can't kill," he said. "Try as you may, you can't step over that line and do it. You yearn for it but can't make take that first bite. That's what drives you insane, that's why you seek vengeance. Is this why you need to find him?"

"Yes," I said.

"What you don't realize is that he messed with some major mojo," he said. "That's why you can't do it, why you can't kill."

"What do you mean?"

"He had enough," he said. "He wasn't supposed to turn anyone else but he turned you, too. That's why it got all fucked up. It's almost like you're the greater good."

"That's bullshit," I said. "I'm not the greater good."

"No," he said. "You're not but you are the beginning of the end."

"This is bullshit," I said and jumped up.

He grabbed my hand and pulled me back down. "No, it's not. Well, maybe it is, who knows? This is just what I've heard and you know how vamps like to embellish."

"Whatever," I said.

He shrugged. "Whatever it means, it means our kind is dying when one of us turns someone who can't survive, who can't drink the blood from a gushing vein. It's a ripple effect and our kind will slowly die out. And it started with you."

That made me feel really bad. I wasn't special after all. I was the beginning of the end. I stared at him and said, "What can I do?"

"Turn someone," he said.

"I can't do that!"

"And that's why we'll all die," he said softly. "Not that I care much. Forever is a long fucking time. I've been around for two centuries. It gets so tedious sometimes."

I rolled my eyes.

"But it's the beginning of the end," he said. "All the myth and folklore, that's all we will be in a few years."

"I don't believe you," I said.

"Well, it is just a rumor," he said.

Just then it occurred to me what he was doing. "Are you making all this up?"

"Yeah," he said, smiling. "I wanted to fuck with you a little."

"Why?"

"Cause I'm evil," he said and grinned, well, evilly.

I had an urge to slap him but I didn't. He was strong and would have beaten the hell out of me if I had.

"Sorry," he said. "Like I said, I'm bored. But I have heard about you and I did want to meet you. Sorry that you can't kill."

"You are such a prick," I said. "I knew not to talk to you. All you vamps are assholes."

"Takes one to know one," he said and gave me a knowing look.

"Fuck you."

"Come on," he said and laughed a little. "Stop being such a downer. That's what's wrong with the world. Everyone is so down, so full of themselves."

"Well, it wasn't you that got left, it was me."

He nodded. "That's true."

I decided to ask his opinion as he had been, at one time, a man. "Why do you think he left me?"

He eyed me and picked up his beer. "Maybe he's just an asshole. You are a hot chick, you know?"

"Thanks," I said dryly. "Let me ask you this. Why do you think I can't kill?"

He shrugged. "I don't know, really. Hey, I know, there's this witch—"

"I've already been to her," I said. "She was a bitch."

"She wouldn't help you?"

"No, she just wanted to mind-fuck me a little," I said. "She hates vamps."

He nodded. "Lots of people do and with good reason."

I sighed and stood. "Well, it's been nice talking to you but I have to go."

"Say hi to Hugo for me," he said and waved at me. "Tell him if he's done with you, I'd like a shot."

"Keep dreaming, asshole," I said and started to leave.

"Hey, Lola," he said. "I know where he is."

I turned. "This better not be bullshit."

"It's not," he said. "He's going to be at the riverfront at daylight."

"At daylight?" I asked. "Why?"

He shrugged. "I heard he was going to kill himself."

★ ★ ★ ★ ★

"Shh," he had murmured the last time we were together. "Just be still."

But I couldn't. I couldn't take it. It was too much. The force of his hands was too much. His hands were becoming too much. The intensity of his hands was taking me over. I squirmed and had to get away from him.

"Don't touch me anymore," I hissed and tried to get away from him. "Please, Hugo, I can't stand it anymore."

He didn't let up and kept at me, touching me, draining me, forcing me to feel his power, his dominance. He was forcing me to feel even though it was torture. He was as close to perfection as someone could ever hope to get. I wanted to be just like him and hated that I wasn't.

He gave a sudden thrust that sent me over the edge. The thrust sent my nails clawing into his back. He didn't cry out with pain as my nails sunk into his skin, he moaned. He liked that. He liked it rough and he liked to give it rough.

Afterwards, he'd said, "You know I'll always love you, right, Lola?"

"Yeah," I said. "And I will always love you, Hugo."

He smiled and that smile had assured me that he would, too. And that's why I had to find him. He'd broken his promise.

I sat on the bed of the hotel and thought about that time, that last time we'd made love. It had gone on all night.

I glanced at the clock on the nightstand. It was almost five in the morning. It was time to leave. It was time to face him. It was time to kill.

I got up and went to my suitcase and pulled the troll's blood out. This would supposedly keep me alive during the daylight. I thought about the troll, the first in a long line I'd questioned and begged for answers. But they didn't have my answers. Hugo did. And he was going to give them to me before he died.

I went to the door, opened it and walked out. I didn't want to be late.

Not the killing kind.

He was waiting for the sun to come up; he was waiting to die. He was at the riverfront, sitting in the thick fog, staring out at it as it consumed the river and made it look like one big hunk of misty fog instead a moving body of water. He sat quietly, calmly, even in his last hours. He didn't want to rush it and he didn't want anything to spoil it.

Well, too bad.

"I know you're there," he said. "Come out and bring your wrath."

I cringed. I'd tracked him down. I felt bad about doing it.

"Come on," he said. "Come now."

I felt in my pocket for the troll's blood. It was there. I was ready. I stepped out and revealed myself to him. He glanced at me and smiled. I almost smiled back, mesmerized by his beauty, by his presence. I stopped myself just in time.

"As always," he said. "You take my breath away, beautiful. If I had any to take, that is."

I didn't chuckle at his dry humor. I didn't say anything at all. I just stood there and wondered if I had the nerve to go though with it.

"Come on," he said and turned to me. "Let me have it. Tell me what a worthless, evil bastard I am."

I just stood there, unable to speak. Unable to do anything but try to contain myself from running and falling on him and kissing him. I wanted to kiss him so bad it hurt but I didn't much want to kill him. Maybe we could have sex first and get it done with, then I'd be able to do it.

"You won't," he muttered, shaking his head. "You'll never be able to go through with it, Lola. Or have you forgotten that you're not the killing kind?"

"Fuck you, Hugo," I said.

"Ah, she is pissed off," he said. "Come on, girl, give it old Hugo, tell him how he let you down."

I glared at him. "Fuck you."

"Ah, passion, anger," he said, standing. "So much passion and anger coming from such a small person."

"Shut up!" I yelled.

"Then do it," he said. "Bring your wrath, stake me! That way I won't waste time waiting for the sun to come out."

"I just want to know why," I said calmly.

"Why what?"

"You know what," I hissed.

"No, I really don't," he said causally. "Refresh my memory."

"Why did you leave me?"

"Oh, come on," he said. "That's the obvious question Lola. Why not ask me something I don't have the answer to?"

"Fuck you," I hissed, seething. "I just want to know why."

He shrugged.

I began to get angry, so angry I *could* have staked him. I stomped over to him and hissed, "Why did you do that to me, you worthless fuck? You left me there to wither away and die!"

"I'd left you before," he said. "And you never died."

"But you'd never left a note before," I hissed. "Why? Tell me why you left me there like that."

He stared at me, a little sadly, and said, "Because I couldn't stand to see what I'd made you."

"Then why did you do it?"

"I couldn't help myself," he muttered. "I loved you so much."

"Loved?" I asked. "You don't love me anymore?"

He stared at me, so sadly. "I do love you, it's just that I realized you were different and I'd made you into something you weren't."

"And what's that?"

"A killer who can't kill," he said. "Someone who doesn't want to kill."

"And why do you think I can't kill?"

"It's a mystery," he said. "No one knows. No one ever will. You're an anomaly."

I didn't like being an anomaly.

He stared at me. "It could have been so great, our love affair. But then…yeah. Maybe it just wasn't meant to be."

"It's not my fault," I said.

"Perhaps not," he said. "And what is this shit I hear about you robbing blood banks? Wouldn't it just be easier to kill? You're not a real vampire, you can't be."

"Wait a minute," I said. "Did you leave me so I'd have to kill? So that I'd be forced to kill?"

He stepped back and said, "Yeah, I did. But it's not in you and that's a disappointment. I should have never turned you."

"So you just run away?" I asked. "How many girls have you turned since you left? What have you been doing?"

"What have I been doing?" he snapped. "I've been looking for a cure, that's what I've been doing! Not that I found one! Not that there *is* one!'

"There's no cure for being a vampire," I snapped back.

"No," he said. "Not for me, for you."

I stumbled back.

"It could have been so great, baby," he said, almost in a pleading voice. "Me and you out there, doing it every night.

But then it turned into something I didn't like. I wanted you to be like me and I guess I was disappointed that you weren't."

"But it's not all about the killing," I said. "You killed enough for both of us! We could have gone on like that."

"You could have," he said. "I couldn't."

I blanched but said, "But you broke my heart."

"It's not your heart that's talking," he said. "It's your pride."

He was right. My pride had been hurt by his leaving, just as it had been hurt by my husband leaving, too. It was hard to take, to know, that someone just didn't want to be with you. It made me crazy, that foolish pride, but I couldn't do anything about it. But his words made me cringe. If I was still capable of embarrassment, I would have blushed. But I wasn't so I didn't. I would have rather died than give him the satisfaction.

"I just wanted to find something," he said. "And see if we could get you cured. That's why I left."

Even though I felt pathetic for saying this, I had to, "No, you left because I'm not good enough."

He stared at me, looking incredibly sad and said, "No, I left you because it was killing me to see what I'd done to you."

"You liar," I said.

"No," he replied. "I'm not lying."

I stood there and stared at him. I couldn't kill him; I'd never be able to. But I couldn't do without him. We were too connected. He was my strength, my life, my breath. I had to have him even if he didn't want me.

"I do want you," he murmured and stepped in close to me. "I want you so badly it scares me. Maybe that's why I left. The love you give me is so intense, it's frightening. You love me, Lola, I know that. But you love me too much. It's scary, even for an old vamp like me."

I turned my head up and he pressed his lips against mine. Then he kissed me and everything dissolved, all the bad feelings. I was home again, home with him, and I was alive. I was there, standing there being kissed by the only man I'd ever truly loved. I couldn't live without him, just as I could never kill him.

He pulled away and smiled gently at me.

"So now are you going to kill yourself?" I asked. "Go up in flames?"

He smiled. "I haven't decided. I just started that rumor to give all the old bastards something to talk about. Have to keep them guessing, you know?"

I nodded. I knew.

"Come sit with me," he said and held out his hand. "Let's do this together, Lola."

We sat there for a long time, until the sun came up. But we didn't explode as we'd both taken our potions, the troll's blood. When neither of us burned, we turned to each other and smiled and felt the sun on our faces for the first time in a long time. It felt good and, for a moment, I felt warm again.

"We can try again tomorrow," he said.

I took his hand. "Or we can just call the whole thing off."

"We can do that," he said. "But let's get out of New Orleans. It's so clichéd."

I nodded, then said, "I finally figured it out, Hugo."

"What?"

"Why I tried to kill myself that one time."

His eyebrows shot up for and instant and he said, "And why was that?"

"Because I couldn't breathe," I said. "I felt so suffocated, numb, as I told you. I was scared of life. But not having it scared me more. And that's when I realized I had to have my breath, at least until you took it away."

"But I always give it back, don't I?" he asked.

I smiled. Yeah, he always did. He wasn't only my breath, but he was my song, the song that played over and over in my head and made me smile. And he'd been waiting on me to find him, even if he had run. He knew as well as I did that without each other, we were halves, unwhole. With each other, we were one, one together, one always, always alone. It was in that isolation that we came together. It was there that each of us could finally breathe.

# Book Two.

I Married a Vampire

The monster.

I was leaving work late, as usual. It was Thursday and the security guard stopped and asked if I would like him to walk me to my car.

"No, thanks," I said and smiled. "I'll be fine."

He nodded. "Be careful."

"Will do," I replied and walked out into the dark Atlanta night. I walked down to the street corner and pressed the "walk" button and waited. Just as the light changed, I heard something behind me. I looked around and studied the dark alley. There was nothing there. I turned back to the light and hurried across the street before it changed.

After I got to the other side and was nearing the parking garage, I definitely heard something behind me. I stopped and looked and could have sworn I saw someone duck into a doorway. I suddenly became aware of my surroundings and became very nervous. I hurried up. The parking garage was only a few yards away. I heard the noise again and increased my pace, almost into a jog. I looked behind me and saw a man, a tall, dark man and he was coming after me. No, he was coming *for* me and he was going to do God knows what.

I wished I had let the security guard walk me to my car.

My fight or flight instinct took over and I ran as fast as I could up the street, even though I was wearing heels and it was difficult. I soon forgot about the car and just focused on trying to find an unlocked building or a person who could help me. I looked behind me to see that he was gaining on me. I screamed. He got closer and chased me down a dark alley and there I came to a dead-end.

I turned around and faced him. He was glaring at me, as if he had a personal vendetta against me. The way he looked at me made me feel as though he could tear me from limb to limb without a thought. And he probably could.

"Stay away from me!" I screamed and rummaged in my purse for my pepper spray, then held it on him. "Stay away!"

He disregarded my words and kept walking, very slowly, to where I stood. Then he knocked the pepper spray out of my hand. I shivered as he grabbed me. He was going to kill me.

"Please," I begged. "Don't do this. Please, I'll—"

"Shut up," he grunted.

I shut up and stared into his dark blue eyes and then at his body, his lean and muscular body. Why was a guy like this chasing girls? He could get a girl—any girl—he wanted. He didn't have to do this, so why was he?

Just then his face changed and it changed into this mean, weird looking thing. It was still his face, only more distorted, more vicious. He looked like a monster. Then I realized that he *was* a monster! As I studied him closer I could see the fangs in his mouth, sharp to the touch, ready to sink into my throat and suck the life's blood out of me.

"Oh, God!" I screamed. "OH GOD!"

He grinned evilly and then shook his head and the monster face disappeared and was replaced by his other face, the handsome face. That terrified me more than the other face and that was because it was deceptive.

He leaned in and pressed his cold lips against mine. I struggled as he tried to kiss me. I beat against his chest and pushed him away but there wasn't much I could do but give in. And, as I submitted, I felt relief wash over me and I felt something else, too. I wanted this and I wanted it more than I'd ever wanted anything in my life. I wanted what he was going to do to me next but the thought didn't disturb me. It just propelled me into the next moment.

My lips softened and he began to kiss me, eat at my lips, suck on them. His hand was under my skirt and he was ripping the panties from my body. I tried to get away but then I didn't want to. He was touching me, playing with me, teasing me, making me want it. And want it, I did. I wanted it so badly, even if I had to take it from him.

"Don't," I said but didn't mean it as he began to suck at my throat. "Please stop."

He didn't respond and continued to lick and suck at my throat and then he ripped my shirt open and devoured my breasts. He flicked his tongue across my nipple before sucking it into his mouth. He squeezed my breast with one hand while the other was between my legs, playing with my pussy. I couldn't take much more of this. I was going to explode with orgasm if he didn't stop. *I was going to... Oh, there, don't stop, right there... I was going to...I was going to heaven.* I had to have it. I had to have his finger on me, teasing me, bringing out the best I had. And then I had it. I exploded with orgasm and it took my breath away. And then, when it was over, I wanted more where that came from.

"Oh, God!" I moaned. "Fuck me!"

He pushed me up against the wall and I wrapped my legs around his waist and he shoved his hard cock into me and started to fuck me. I sucked him into me and rode him like he was riding me. I couldn't get enough of him, of this moment; even if it was wrong, it felt right. It felt right to have him do that to me, to fuck me in an alley. *What would he do after we were done?*

I began to come right then, as he was coming. I couldn't get enough of it and wanted it so bad, just like I wanted him. The orgasm exploded inside me and I threw my head back and screamed with delight, almost with pain because it was so good it was almost unbearable.

"Oh, yeah," he said. "Oh God!"

I met him as he pumped into me and fucked that orgasm right out of his body. We kept fucking until he was spent and I could barely move.

"Umm," he moaned and kissed me gently, sliding his tongue over my lips before he pushed it into my mouth. He pulled away and smiled at me.

"Oh, baby," I moaned and grinned back. "That was so good."

"It was, wasn't it?" he asked and seemed pleased with himself.

"Do the scary face again!" I exclaimed.

He groaned. "Oh, come on, Keri."

"*Please!*" He groaned again and did it. Oh! He was *so* scary when he did that. And so sexy. I touched the bottom of his teeth and said, "How do you keep them so sharp?"

"I don't have to keep them sharp, they just stay that way," he said and shook his head, going back to his normal face.

"Oh," I said. "Next time I want you to chase me in the park and we can have sex on a bench."

"Can't we just do it in a bed every once in a while?"

I studied him and replied, "What's the fun in that?"

✱ ✱ ✱ ✱ ✱

I didn't even know he was a real vampire at first. We met at a bar—a salsa bar. He was there with some skanky ho. I was there with my best friend, Claire, who had just gone through a bad breakup. We were there to try to cheer her up but as soon as I laid eyes on him, I forgot about her, much to her chagrin. But then she said, "I know you like him, so go."

"I've seen him before," I muttered.

"Oh?" she said. "Where?"

I turned to her. "In the butcher's shop."

"Why were you in a butcher's shop?"

"I was buying meat there, why else?" I said. "But, yeah, I've seen him before."

"So go see him again," she said and gave me a little smile. "Just go."

Typically, he remembered it another way. In his memory, he was at the bar—still with the skanky ho—and he saw me. He said I mesmerized him and he couldn't take his eyes off me. He said it was like we were caught in a dream and it was a nice, warm one. I caught him staring and snapped, "What the fuck are you looking at?" And then, according to him, I stomped off.

His memory was more accurate, I am ashamed to admit. But then again, I had a girl crying on my shoulder about what absolute bastards men can be. However, he didn't give up on me and sent a drink over to my table. Then I noticed he was *really* cute and the rest is history. Well, actually, I continued to ignore him for the rest of the night, which was probably what sealed his obsession with me. What was it with guys always wanting the one chick who doesn't acknowledge their existence? I actually didn't talk to him until a few days later when I saw him again at the same butcher shop I'd mentioned before. That's when things started cooking.

As I said, I didn't know he was a vampire and that's because I didn't know vampires existed. But they do. They're out there. But they're not as mean and as evil as people let on. Well, some of them are, but my man wasn't. He was a real sweetheart. Well, sometimes he was a real sweetheart. Right now, he was a pain in my ass.

"You asshole!" I yelled. "You left the toilet seat up again!"

He didn't respond.

"Hey!" I yelled.

"Sorry!" he yelled back. "For God's sake, I'm trying to sleep here!"

"Whatever," I grunted and slammed the toilet seat down. I went to the vanity, put some toothpaste on my toothbrush and started brushing my teeth. As I did so, I stared at myself in the mirror. I looked good. Yeah, I was *hot*. It must have been all that good sex I was having or something but my skin, though freckled, just glowed. My eyes were a bit brighter, too, a really nice bright blue. And my dark brown hair never looked shinier. I grinned at myself in the mirror, loving that fresh-faced-just-fucked look I had. My body, too, was better than ever. I was short, sure, but very trim and I had a great ass.

Good sex also gave a girl good confidence. Good sex could conquer all. I really was beginning to believe that.

I winked at myself before turning on the shower but then something caught my eye. I stepped over and peered, then I screamed. It was a dead rat lying next to the vanity. I screamed again and began to dance with disgust and fear. "Oh, God! *Duke!*"

He responded this time with a, "What the fuck is it now?"

"There's a dead rodent in the bathroom!" I screamed.

"Oh, shit," he muttered and I heard him stomping towards the bathroom. He stopped next to me and stared at the dead rat. "Where the bloody hell did that thing come from?"

"I don't know," I said. "Isn't it yours?"

"Mine?!" he snapped. "What the fuck does that mean? Why do you assume that just because I'm a vampire that I eat things like that?"

I stared at him. Thank God it wasn't his. Even so, sometimes being married to a vampire was such a pain in the ass. No, most times it was.

Yeah, you heard me. I married a vampire. The whole, "Allow me to suck you neck, dahling," thing. The whole big teeth that come down when they're about to bite their prey thing. The whole dressed in black thing.

He grabbed a towel, threw it on top of the rat and then retrieved it from the floor. Then he disappeared out the door with it. *He'd better be taking it to the garbage chute,* I thought. I listened and he was back in about a minute. Good.

"Where did it come from?" I asked.

"It must have been Ted's," he said. "Next time he does that, he's in for it."

Ugh. Ted's his stupid demon friend. He has horns and everything. He was really nasty but I guess that goes without saying if he eats rats. I wished Duke would stop hanging out with demons like Ted, but he always says, "We go way back." Duke was a very loyal friend.

Yeah, that's his real name, Duke. He's so damned old that he had a name like Duke. And get this—he doesn't even have a last name or at least not one that he can remember anymore. He had to make one up when we got married and guess what he picked? Longtooth. Yeah, Longtooth. I'm Mrs. Longtooth. How awful is that? Well, it's probably better than being Mrs._____.

Good thing I decided to keep my maiden name.

We got along for the most part, but we fought a lot too. So much that I'd been trying to divorce the son of a bitch since the day we got hitched. It's just wasn't working out. We fought constantly and when weren't fighting, we were fucking, which was good but as soon as the afterglow wore off, it was back to work. I complained about it all the time.

My mother said, "You're still newlyweds. Work it out. It gets better."

"You and dad still fight like you're going to kill each other, though."

"Yeah," she said. "That never goes away."

I didn't even want to marry him. Not really. No, I guess I did. But—but!—I didn't realize vampires existed. When he told me he was one, I almost fell over. But then I didn't really believe him. However, after a while and after witnessing things such as Ted and the dead rat, I came to realize vampires are quite real and can be quite scary. And, also, they're excellent lovers.

We'd only known each other about a year. We had this really sweet whirlwind romance and then one day he popped the question. I should have known something was up when he gave me a skull and crossbones ring instead of a diamond.

I was like, "What is this shit?"

He just stared at the ring, then at me, wondering what he did wrong. "I...uh... Don't you like it?"

No, I didn't like it. I took it but I never liked it. And I certainly never wore the damned thing. He acted all pouty about it, too. But I couldn't wear that ugly ring to work. They'd think I'm a devil worshiper or something! And I'm in real estate so you could see where that might be a problem.

He never did anything right.

We lived in a fabulous apartment near downtown Atlanta. I moved into it before I met Duke. It was one of those rare finds in real estate that are just too good to be true. In this case, though, it hadn't been and I snatched it right up. One day I wanted to build my dream house but right now, this was good. We had plenty of room and a nice view. We were close to a park. We could walk to bars and restaurants. It was great. Duke liked it because the windows had these heavy-duty shades on them. If they're closed during the daytime, it almost looks like night.

When I saw Duke at a butcher's shop the second time, after we'd seen each other at the salsa bar, I should have known something was up with him. However, it was like something was pushing us together. It was very odd, like fate or destiny or something.

Of course, I was there on an errand for my mom, who wanted some more steaks and asked if I would pick them up for her on my way to a family function. He was there buying steaks, like me, and blood. Of course, I didn't know he was buying blood. I thought he was just some strange guy dressed all in black who was so beyond cute I could barely hold myself off him.

We locked eyes and I was hooked. Then I stepped back and got a good look at him, especially at his clothes. He was dressed like someone from a really old movie, the silent kind. Then I thought better of the lust I was feeling and turned away from him.

However, he tapped me on the shoulder. "Hullo. Didn't I see you at the bar the other night?"

I tried to ignore him but his voice intrigued me. He had an English accent which was so sexy to me. He said "hello" like "hullo!" It was so sexy.

He tapped me on the shoulder again. "I'm Duke. Who are you?"

I turned to him and said, "I'm not interested."

"In what?" he asked, a little confused. "Did you at least like the drink?"

"I don't drink Bloody Marys very often," I said. "But it was one of the better ones I've had."

He smiled and held out his hand. "I'm Duke."

I hesitated for a second, but then shook his hand. As our hands touched, I felt an electricity I'd never felt before. I gasped and stared up into his eyes. He stared back and nodded slightly. And, the next thing I know, we were married.

I think he mesmerized me at the butcher's shop. (At least that's what I tell him when I'm mad at him which was most of the time.) Maybe I didn't even like him that much. Maybe it was all because of his vampire tricks. Needless to say, whatever he did worked. However, it's been work for me ever since.

It's been hard though, real hard. I had to do so much work on him it's unbelievable. First of all, his clothes—God-awful! I had to change that right off the bat. So much black and tweed and, on top of that, he had an earring! That had to go. I wasn't walking around in public with him looking like that.

Secondly, his manners. Specifically, his inability to give up human blood. He was always eying other people in this very unusual way, the way humans look at steaks or cupcakes. I told him that if we were together, he had to give that up. He said he'd get it under control and he did. He'd better not be lying either. Although, sometimes he did come home smelling of cheap wine and then I read about some hobo disappearing.

Thirdly, he was lazy. He wouldn't work. I thought he could get a job of some kind but he was happy to spend his days playing video games and waiting for me to come home. That was definitely going to change if I didn't divorce him.

Fourthly, the fights. Oh, my God, we got into some major fights. They were outrageous and the neighbors always complained. Of course, by the time the superintendent got there to tell us to calm down, we were inevitably having wild monkey sex.

Ah, the sex. That's the only thing that kept us together, I think. We had really good sex. Only trouble was, after the sex was over, the fights started again. It's a vicious cycle—fight, sex, fight, sex…

Right now I wasn't worried about fighting and I wasn't worried because he had come into the bathroom and stepped into the shower with me. He turned me around to him and just stared at me. He had that look in his eye. He always looked so handsome and he looked even better than that when he was naked. I could have eaten him alive.

He cocked his head to the side and grinned. His teeth were perfect, straight and white. His nice, smooth face had a glow to it. It might have been the soft lighting in the bathroom that made him look that way, though. He was usually a lot paler.

He began to kiss me, soft kisses as the warm water beat down on us. I smiled as he kissed and felt so alive and so wanted. It was nice to feel that wanted. It was sometimes unbelievable to me that another person could make me feel that way.

I began to shiver in delight as he caressed my naked breasts then bent to kiss them. As I threw my head back, a soft moan escaped his lips and I found my hands in hair, playing with it and holding his head steady.

"I love you so much, baby," he moaned and came back to my lips.

"I love you, too," I moaned back and received his wet, hot kiss. Um, this was the best. It was so the best. I never wanted it to end.

His hands were making their way along my body, sending the warmth up between my legs. My nipples were erect and wanted his lips on them but at the same time, I yearned for him to put his hand between my legs. I pushed out my chest for him to get the hint, then he did and bent down to take a nipple into his mouth while his hand squeezed my other breast.

Ah, that felt *so* good.

In no time, he was getting more concentrated, more desperate with his touches. He was ready to fill me. So he pulled me out of the tub and pushed me down on the floor and fell on top of me. I opened my legs and he settled in, giving me all of himself, and he had quite a lot to give.

It didn't take long before the fucking took over us and all we could do was hold on tight and press up against each other. I wrapped my legs around his waist and pushed him in more deeply inside of me, wanting it all, all of it and wanting it now.

"Harder," I moaned.

He did it harder, slamming into me. Soon, I couldn't take it anymore and I just gave myself over to it and the orgasm erupted inside of me. I bit down on his shoulder as I came and came hard. It was almost too much and I was heading into overload. I thought for an instant that I might explode, just as the orgasm had exploded inside of me.

He was right behind me, coming and coming hard. As he came, he fell down on top of me and sighed with satisfaction, almost with relief, as if the lust inside of him was too much to bear.

I turned his face to mine and kissed him. He kissed back, smiling slightly as he did so. This was the best part of being married.

As soon as it was over, we were back to fighting again. Ain't love grand?

Big Duke.

One of our biggest recurring fights was over money and Duke's inability to work. Or, rather, his refusal to work.

"You are going to have to get a job!" I yelled at him.

"Why do you always have to ruin breakfast?" he asked and waved his hands over the kitchen table. "I thought we were getting along today."

"We're not going to get along until you get a job."

"Doing what?" he asked. "What can *I* do?"

I just stared at him.

"Need I remind you that I was born a long time ago," he said. "Any skills I picked up when I was alive are null and void. Also, I'm a vampire and vampires and sun don't mix. Most jobs are during the day."

"You could work at a convenience store," I said. "They have third shifts."

"I am not working at one of those," he scoffed. "It's too dangerous."

I groaned. I don't know why I didn't just give up. Why didn't I just give up on him? He was never going to be normal.

"What's normal anyway?" he said. "No one knows."

"Stop reading my mind, fuckhead," I said.

"Don't call me fuckhead," he said, getting agitated. "I *hate* that."

I rolled my eyes but didn't push it. "Well, you could work stacking boxes in a warehouse somewhere."

"I'd be too tempted to kill everyone in there after a few hours. Besides, I tried that once."

I let that one slide. With Duke, one should do that. You never knew what kind of story he might tell but you could always be assured that it would give you nightmares, even if all that was "behind him" now.

"Well," I said, considering. "You could drive a truck. You could drive a delivery truck."

"I'd go crazy," he said. "Besides, you have to have a special driver's license."

Oh, God, it was hopeless. I eyed him and felt all the anger and frustration building. The fight erupted before I knew what was happening and we were at each other's throats. We yelled and screamed and called each other names and then the phone rang. It was the superintendent and he said he if we didn't "Shut the fuck up!" he would have us evicted. I told him I was sorry and that we'd do better.

I slammed the phone down and glared at Duke. "It's all your fault."

"It always is," he groaned.

"I have to get to work," I said. "Somebody has to!"

I stomped out of the apartment, slamming the door on my way out, and headed to the parking garage. I was going to kill him one day.

I should *kill him!*

I turned back around and headed to the apartment.

No, I can't do that.

I turned back around and headed towards my car. But why shouldn't I? He's supposed to be dead already! He was, like, way over a hundred years old, maybe two. Just exactly how old was he anyway? Maybe he was about two-hundred. He said he was turned in the early 1800s but then again, he always got his dates mixed up, so he could have been turned in the 1700s. Either way, he was damn old.

Yeah, I should just go ahead and do it. I could stake him in no time and still get to work on time.

I turned back around and headed home.

Shit! I couldn't kill the son of a bitch, though no one would notice or even care if I did. But why couldn't I? Because I loved him. I hated myself for doing that sometimes. Why did I have to fall in love with a vampire? *Why?!*

But I did feel kind of bad. I glanced at my watch. I should go up and apologize. I didn't want to ruin his day. I didn't tell myself I was going because I knew we'd probably have sex. I was like an addict with him or something.

I went back in to find him on the couch watching TV. He stared at me as I stepped in front of him, blocking his view.

"Get out of the way," he said. "There's this interesting news-bit on right now."

"Duke," I said. "I just wanted to come back and apologize for being such a bitch."

"You didn't have to do that," he said, looking around me at the TV. "Sweetheart, please move. I'm watching the news."

I grabbed the remote and turned it off. "Fuck the news," I said and straddled him. "And fuck me."

He grinned and ran his hands up my sides. "Oh, you didn't come back to apologize. You came back for a little more of Big Duke."

I groaned. It should be no surprise that he had a name for his penis and that name was Big Duke. He had promised me that he would never refer to it like that again. But he always managed to slip it in occasionally.

I didn't want to start a fight, so I bent down and brushed my lips against his. He responded by grabbing my head and kissing me hard. Soon, we were heavy petting and were just about to get to the good part when someone knocked on the door.

We stopped and glanced over at it.

"It might be important," Duke said.

I groaned and got up and went to the door and opened it. And there stood one of his loser friends, the demon called Ted. The one who had left the dead rat in my bathroom. I didn't like him much, but then again, I don't think anyone liked him. For what it's worth, he couldn't stand me either. Humans and demons rarely, if ever, get along.

Ted cleared his throat and said, "Uh, is Duke here?"

I rolled my eyes and opened the door and waved my hand at Duke. Duke jumped up and shouted, "Hullo, Ted!"

"Hey!" he said and scratched at one of his horns.

I cringed.

"How's it going?" Duke asked and gave him a quick hand shake.

"Same old, same old," he said and didn't look at me. "Could I see you out in the hall for a moment?"

I rolled my eyes. This Ted guy was the worst. Well, first of all, he wasn't a guy; he was a bona fide demon. He was always coming up with some scheme for them to make a quick buck. That's one reason Duke refused to get a job because these little schemes of his and Ted's always "kept him afloat".

Duke had a lot of weird friends. Once, just after we got married, I was sorting through my clothes, trying to find a work outfit and getting frustrated in the process.

"I don't have anything to wear!" I yelled towards Duke's general direction on the bed.

"You have loads of clothes," he said. "So stop bitching."

"Go to hell," I said. As soon as the words were out of my mouth there was a noise and the rack fell down in the closet.

I leapt back to see this young guy standing there. He was saying, "Sorry, sorry. I meant to come in the front door but... Just so sorry."

"Who the hell are you?" I screeched. "Duke!"

Duke jumped up, then grinned. "Hullo! What are you doing here?"

I watched as they gave each other friendly smiles. I asked, "Who's he?"

"A guy I killed almost fifty years ago."

"Oh, I'm sorry," I said to the ghost.

"Why are you sorry?" he asked. "I've never been happier. I get to float around all day and haunt people. I even get to creep out this one chick I wanted to date but hated me." He chuckled happily and stared up at the ceiling. "Now that's fun."

"Huh," was all I could think of to say.

"Yeah," Duke said. "Sal here drops by to see me every decade or so. He haunts me, too."

"Part of the job," Sal said dryly. "I would shake your hand but I can't. Being a ghost and all." He chuckled again.

I nodded, not knowing what to say, which was unusual for me. Shit like that happened all the time. It was almost an everyday occasion. But at least I haven't seen Sal since. He only haunts every decade or so, as Duke explained. He's on a tight schedule.

Just then, Duke and Ted came back in laughing and Duke kissed me on the cheek and shoved a thick envelope in my hand.

"What's this?" I asked.

"Compensation," Duke said proudly.

I eyed him before opening the envelope to find a shitload of money. "Where did this come from?"

"Uh, you know, that deal I was telling you about," Duke said. "It finally panned out."

"I have no idea what you're talking about," I told him.

He stared at me and said slowly, "It's a deal we had cooking and I don't know if you want to know the *details*... However, if you would like me to tell you exactly—"

"Say no more," I said quickly and held up my hand.

"Let's celebrate," Ted said. "Pick up some hot chicks or something."

"I'm standing right here, Ted," I said and rolled my eyes. "I'm Duke's wife. He's not allowed to pick up hot chicks. He's *married*."

"Oh, right," he said. "I mean, I know that, Keri. I know he's married. I didn't mean for him to pick up some hot chicks or whatever. I meant—"

"Don't explain," I said and pushed the thought of any woman kissing or doing anything else with Ted out of my mind before it permanently turned me off sex. I turned to Duke and said, "I have to go to work."

"Have a good day, sweetheart," he said and kissed my cheek. "Need me to walk you to your car?"

"Sure," I said and grinned at him.

Of course, "walking" me to my car usually entailed having sex with me on top of it. I don't know why we did it, but we started kissing in the elevator and then we were on top of my car, doing it. Good thing that most people in the building had already gone to work.

"Love you," he said after we were finished.

I nodded, buttoned my blouse and said, "Remember that mom wants us to come to dinner tonight."

"Will do," he said and kissed me before heading to the elevator.

I watched him go with a smile. Life was good sometimes. I couldn't wait to get home and fuck him again.

Half-moon.

"Duke!" my mom exclaimed as she opened up her front door. "How good to see you!"

Of course, she ignored me and pulled Duke into a big hug. My mom loved Duke, which was weird because she hated every other guy I'd brought home.

"Hi, mom," I said.

"Keri," she said and smiled at me. "How are you?"

It didn't escape me that she treated Duke like a son and me like a daughter-in-law. I let it go because it was just too weird to think about and I had enough weirdness in my life, what with being married to a vampire, having demons and ghosts visit my apartment and all that.

"Come in, come in," she said. "Duke, you go sit with Harold in the living room. Keri and I will finish up dinner in the kitchen."

Duke grinned and joined my father, who liked him about as much as my mother did, and I went to help with dinner.

As I chopped vegetables for the salad, I said, "Mom he still won't get a job."

"Oh, who cares?" she said. "He's such a nice boy."

"Mom, he's a vampire," I said. "And he's not a boy, he's old. Older than you. And grandpa!"

"Oh, stop saying that," she said and tutted me.

I rolled my eyes. She didn't believe me. She thought I was making all this up just to put Duke down. My mom loved Duke so much it was almost sickening. She didn't care if he didn't work or if he slept all day or, even, if he was a vampire. He was a, "Nice boy." And, apparently, that's all that mattered. Maybe she liked him because he was old-fashioned and polite around her. Maybe I was jealous because he got better treatment than I did and I was her child not just some random person one of her kids drug into the family.

"Besides," she said. "You make enough money for both of you."

"That's not the point," I said. "He's a bum."

"Bum?" she said. "He's not a bum. If he lived in a cardboard box and drank cheap wine all day, he'd be a bum. Oh, can he eat chicken?"

I nodded. "He can eat anything, he just prefers blood."

She considered. "I don't have any of that."

I rolled my eyes. "Mom, listen, if you think it's weird that I'm married to a vampire, just say so and I'll divorce him."

"Why would you want to divorce him?" she asked, almost appalled. "He's the best man you've ever had."

"He's a vampire!" I shouted. "It's not normal! The relationship we have is wrong!"

I heard a noise and looked over to see Duke standing in the doorway. He looked a little upset, then he smiled at my mom and asked for a couple of beers.

"Of course," mom said and fetched him two beers from the fridge.

He left, but not before throwing me a look of hurt. I felt bad. I was bad. I was worse than he was. Why couldn't I just accept who he was? Why did I think I had to change him?

"You shouldn't be so mean," mom said. "You're hurting his feelings."

I groaned. It was going to be a long night.

"I just think he's great, that's all, honey," she said.

I stared at her. She was almost glowing. She looked almost human. Then it occurred to me what was *really* going on and I was going to kill Duke over it.

★ ★ ★ ★ ★

"You mesmerized my parents!" I accused as we drove away.

"What?!" Duke exclaimed.

I turned to him. "You did! You mesmerized them into liking you!"

"No!" he said, shaking his head. Then he sighed and said, "Well, a little."

"I knew it!" I snapped my fingers. "I knew you did that! They've hated every single guy I've ever gone out with. Why did you do that?"

"Because they hated me too, at first."

That was true. They had hated him. But then, they'd come around and started to like him, a little *too* much. This may have been one of the reasons I started to dislike him after we got married. No girl wants her man to be liked by her parents. It makes him seem boring—and a little weird.

I stared at him and said, "Did you mesmerize me when we met?"

"Oh, don't start that now. *You* mesmerized *me*!"

"I'm not a vamp," I said and studied him. "Maybe you're not as good looking as I think because you did mesmerize me."

"Oh, sweetheart," he said. "I *am* this good looking."

I stared at little more and sighed with satisfaction that he was mine because he was, in fact, one hot piece of ass. Damn! He was so damn good looking it should be against the law or something. And he was mine, all mine. But he was still a little shit for mesmerizing my parents.

"You shouldn't have mesmerized my parents, though," I said. "That's not right."

"Sorry," he said. "But how else was I supposed to get along with them? They hated me and your mom was such a bitch. And your dad is such a hard-ass."

He was right about that. He should have grown up with them. My mom was so bad she wouldn't even let me have a boyfriend until after I moved out of the house. No wonder I was warped and ended up with a vampire for a husband. If I thought about it, I could probably convince myself that it really wasn't my fault at all.

Then he did a little accusing his own, "And, besides, you always act like I have the plague or something around them."

"I do not!"

"Yes, you do," he said. "And you always bring up how you're going to divorce me."

I hung my head because it was true. I was an awful person sometimes.

"Why do you always do that?" he asked quietly.

"Do what?" I asked and stared up ahead at the red-light. I looked over at him in the driver's seat. I felt bad about accusing him of mesmerizing my parents, even if he had done it. He only did it because he liked me so much. And he looked really good tonight and so sexy.

"Always saying you're going to divorce me," he said, staring at me. "It hurts my feelings."

"Were you listening to our whole conversation or something?"

"Yeah, I was, but that's not the point," he said. "Is that how you really feel about me?"

I sighed. "It's hard, Duke, to be married to you because of your condition."

"I'm a vampire," he said. "I don't *have* a condition."

"Bullshit," I said. "You can't do things people can do. I can't enjoy the same things I would with a regular guy."

"Like what?" he asked.

"I can't enjoy the sun with you," I said. "We can't even go to the beach and I love the beach!"

"Fine," he muttered, then suddenly did a U-turn in the middle of the street and took a different route.

"What are you doing?" I asked and held onto the door. "Don't wreck my fucking car, Duke!"

"You'll see," he said.

"Tell me where you're going."

He shushed me and shook his head, then drove a few miles to a park. He stopped the car and turned to me.

"Come with me," he said and got out.

I followed him outside and to the park. He held my hand the whole way there and then we went to a small clearing and he said, "Look up at that."

I stared up at the half-full moon. "So?"

"So that's what I have," he said. "I can share it with you. So what if we can't share the sun? Some couples can't even share the same apartment without falling apart."

He was so good at this stuff.

"The moon is ours, Keri," he said and took my hand. "We might not have the sun, but we have the moon. It moves the tides on the ocean, you know?"

I smiled at him.

"Isn't that enough?"

"But," I said. "I'm going to get old and ugly and wrinkly."

"Nah," he said. "Not you."

"Duke, it's a fact. I will."

"Keri," he said and bent down to stare me in the eyes. "You will always, always be beautiful to me."

"Whatever," I said.

"When and if you go," he said. "I'm going, too."

"What do you mean?"

"I've lived," he said. "And you're the best part of any of it and when you pass, I will kill myself. Probably."

"Oh, shut up."

"I mean it," he said. "So, don't think that you could ever be ugly and undesirable to me because you can't. No one has ever made me feel like this."

"But you'll always be young and I'll always get older," I said and sobbed. "Just like in the book *Orlando*."

"What does Florida have to do with this?"

He was such a dumbass! I was referring to the novel by Virginia Wolff! I mean, come on! Of course, it *was* an obscure reference, but so what? He didn't know anything about books or culture and look at how long he'd been around. He was content to just lie around the apartment and sleep or watch TV or play video games. And that's all he ever did! He was living in a sewer before me.

"It was not a sewer," he snapped. "It was *near* the water treatment facility, that's all."

"Stop reading my mind!" I half-yelled.

"Oh, come on," he said and took me in his arms. "We're so lucky baby."

"How's that?"

"We have this," he said and stared up at the moon. "It's all I can give you but it's great. Just take it, okay?"

I had to smile at him. "Okay, I'll take it. But you are going to have to do something about getting a job."

The tease.

"You are so sexy," Duke said. "Dead sexy."

I smiled at him. He was on the couch waiting for me. I loved making him wait.

"Oh, damn," he said. "You look hot."

The good thing about being a newlywed was that the sex was never boring. Also, I enjoyed dressing up and turning my vampire on. I smiled at him and leaned against the wall. He stared at me intently, his eyes not wavering from my body at all. He liked my schoolgirl outfit and the fact that my hair was in braids. He liked the penny loafers and bobby socks, too. He liked me looking like a hot schoolgirl.

"Come here," he said and motioned me over.

"Where?" I teased and pointed. "Over there?"

"Yes, over here," he said.

I bit my bottom lip and walked over to him and got between his legs like a stripper. He smiled at me and I smiled back a little, then ran my hands up and down his legs, slightly scraping my nails against his pants. I suddenly felt a surge of power and that enabled me to really get into it. It enabled me to give my body over to the act of giving my man pleasure. I began to lean in towards him with my whole body, grinding it against his crotch.

His hands were all over me as I moved against him. He wanted me, he wanted to fuck me, but he wanted me to be a little tease first. I was going to give him what he wanted and I was going to torture him beforehand.

I ran my head up and down his body like a cat and he responded by grabbing it and kissing me. We ate at each other's mouths for a moment, taking turns to suck at our tongues and lips. It was a wet, hot intense kiss and got me so hot I wanted to eat him alive. Or dead. Or whatever.

I moved away from his mouth and kissed his face, all of it, even his eyelids, then slid my tongue along his throat before I sucked it. Then I was going down, down towards his cock which was ready and hard, sticking up inside of his pants, forming a tent.

I nibbled and kissed my way down and stuck my head between his legs and started to nibble on his crotch. I took my time to tease him. It worked because a loud moan soon came out of his mouth. He was getting excited. He was losing himself in it. That made me feel strong and sexy.

"Oh, baby," he moaned. "Just put it in your mouth."

I grinned because I had him, literally, by the balls. I unzipped his pants and his dick popped out. It was in my hands and it was long and hard, slightly throbbing as it awaited my mouth. It was ready for me to do what I was going to do, ready to please me if I decided I wanted that. But this was his turn and he was going to get what he wanted.

"You are so hot," he said and ran his hands through my hair.

"Mmm," I moaned.

I rose up and gave him a big, open-mouthed kiss, sucking at his lips before I began to give him a hand job. I gripped it and ran my hands up and down it, lightly fingering the shaft. He moaned and nearly rose up off the couch. I ignored him and concentrated only on his dick, running my hands up and down it, gripping it like a baseball bat.

"That's a little tight," he said. "Ease up just a little."

I eased up and gave him a lighter stroke. He responded by nodding and looking at me like I was the only woman on earth. I *loved* that.

I stared up at him as I stroked and he stared down at me. There was such sexual tension in that stare, it was unbelievable. Such pure sexual energy. It was almost beautiful.

It was time to really get the show on the road. I dropped my mouth to it then and he grunted as my lips made first contact. I went up and down on it, using my hands to grip it as I sucked. The saliva from my mouth made it easier. It was all wet and sexy. Then I forgot about everything else and deep-throated him, then sucked him harder.

He came up off the couch.

"Shh," I said. "Sit still."

"It's hard to," he muttered.

I shook my head at him and went right back down on it, all the way to the end and then back up, again, sucking as hard as I could. I came up for some air, keeping my hands stroking him and said, "Do you like that?"

"It's the best thing in the world, baby," he murmured. "The best feeling in the world."

I grinned and went back down on it, then came back up and said, "It tastes good."

He grinned and nodded. "It feels good, too."

"Mmm," I moaned, sucking it. "Your cock tastes so good, baby."

I was really into it, so much that I was making all kinds of strange noises as I sucked. I realized I was so turned on, I wanted him to fuck me. But not before I was done with this. I wanted to complete this mission. I wanted to give him something he would *never* forget.

I was having such a good time, I didn't even realize he was about to come. It was all about me giving it to him and getting pleasure from giving. I knew he liked the way I sucked him. I sucked him hard, like I was sucking a lollipop.

I was sucking him so hard he was wriggling. He was moaning. He was about to come.

But before I let him come, I totally lost all inhibition. I raised his cock up and licked my way down it to his balls and then I sucked them into my mouth, gently sucking them as I knew too much pressure would hurt him.

"Fuck!" he moaned. "Fuck!"

I gave his balls one last suck, then went back to his cock. I couldn't believe he was still holding it. Maybe because I hadn't told him he could come yet. I was in control. He wasn't about to do anything until I said to.

"Come on now, baby," I said softly. "Come on."

He nodded and I went back to his cock. As I gave one last, hard suck, he erupted and came into my mouth, his white hot cum filling it up. I swallowed and kept sucking until he was dry. I felt some of his cum on the side of my mouth. I licked the corner of my mouth and stared up at him. He stared down at me with an intense look of shock and wonder. I never felt so alive as I did, so loved and so worshipped. He was going to worship me from now on. He would be out of his mind with lust for me from now on. I had him and that was a good feeling.

"I can't believe you just did that," he said in awe. "You are so fantastic."

I grinned and climbed up on him, pushing him back on the couch. I said, "Now your turn."

He grinned back and grabbed me, kissing me so hard I lost my breath. Then his hand began to roam my body, tearing at my clothes until I was completely and totally naked. He flipped us over until I was beneath him and he was back in control. I just lay there and panted, knowing what was coming and wanting it so bad I couldn't take it. I prayed he wouldn't stop.

He didn't. He began to finger me, rubbing me lightly before he pushed one finger inside of me. I arched up and moaned loudly. He kept his thumb on my clit and kept moving it in circles.

"You are so wet," he said and kissed me. "So hot, baby."

I smiled at him. He smiled back and began to kiss his way down my body until he was between my legs and there he pushed his head in and gave me one long and hot lick. I grabbed at his head and wanted more. He gave it to me and began to suck at my entire pussy, using the long strokes I loved. He kept at it until I was moaning with each breath. He didn't move away from me until I grabbed his head and pushed myself into his face, begging him not to stop. I was coming hard and it was a powerful orgasm that took over my entire being. I felt like I was on fire.

"Oh, God, oh, yes," I moaned and grabbed at his dick which was, thankfully, hard again. (That's one good thing about being married to a vampire—they can go all night.) I moaned and wriggled, then shouted, "Fuck me!"

He was on top of me, fucking me, taking me. Using me as I used him. We couldn't have stopped for anything; we were that turned on. I wrapped my legs around his waist and pushed him in as deep as he could get. I felt totally connected with him then; it was just us, fucking and giving each other a pleasure that's unattainable except for an act like this.

But then it hit me, the second orgasm, and I grabbed onto him and sunk my teeth into his shoulder. He cried out, not with pain, but from pleasure, as he came with me. We were slamming into each other, fucking so hard the couch rocked.

"Oh, God," I moaned as I shook with the orgasm. "OH, GOD!"

He grunted and slammed into me a few more times just as my orgasm began to dissipate. Then it was over. He fell on top of me and caught his breath. It took me a few seconds to get my breath back. As I lay there panting, I looked over at him and said, "You're a dirty vamp."

He grinned at me and said, "And you're a dirty girl."

I smiled, very pleased with myself.

He nuzzled my neck and said softly, "That was the best, baby."

I nodded. Yeah. I knew it.

He kissed my cheek. "Thanks."

"You're welcome," I said, then stared at the bite mark I'd left on his shoulder. "Sorry about that."

He glanced at it. "That's okay. In fact, that was hot."

I nodded. "It looks like a vamp bite, doesn't it?"

He shrugged. "Well, it's in the wrong place, but yeah, I guess. A little."

"I'd make a good vampire," I said and kissed the mark.

He stared at me.

"I'd be so hot, I'd be smoking," I said and grinned evilly. "Why don't you turn me?"

"What?"

"Into a vampire," I said. "It would be great, just us two, being vamps. Besides that, I wouldn't have to worry about wrinkles or—"

"Don't you ever say that again," he said angrily.

"Why?" I asked, sitting up.

He glared at me and got up.

"What is it?" I asked.

"You have no idea what kind of pain you have to go through to become a vampire, do you? It can kill people, it's that bad. Plus, you might turn all evil. You might go bad, you know? Not everyone turns out like me."

I scoffed. "Please. Like you're so strong and so good."

"That's not what I meant," he said. "If you died, I'd die."

"Huh?"

He looked away. "Keri, do you know how much I love you? And if I turned you and you died, I'd want to die."

"How sweet," I said and threw my hands around his neck.

"I mean it," he said. "Don't ever mention me turning you again."

"Fine," I grumbled. "But what about when I get old and ugly? You'll still be young and hot."

"You'll never be old or ugly," he said.

"How's that?"

"Because you'll always be beautiful to me even when you're old and ugly."

"You say that now but just wait until my tits sag," I said. "I'm thirty-four, almost thirty-five, now. It might not be long before these puppies head south."

His head jerked up. He hadn't thought about that.

"See?" I said and pointed my finger at him. "And when I'm gone, you can get another girl and live another life. It's not really fair when you get right down to it."

He grabbed my finger and shook his head. "When you croak, I croak."

"Huh?"

"When you die," he said. "I'm going to off myself."

"You said that before," I said. "Are you really serious about this?"

He nodded. "I don't want to live without you."

I grinned at him. He was so good with that stuff. He always knew what to say.

Then he said, "What's for supper?"

I groaned.

Bitter enemies.

Of course, the day after that, we were back to our old selves, fighting like bitter enemies. We were fighting in public, which was always so nice. The evening had started out good. We'd had a late supper at a really nice restaurant, then we'd hit this club downtown I'd loved to come to when I was single. We danced the night away and drank fruity, tropical drinks. It was nice. Soon, it was late and we had to leave the club. So, we went walking around the city, ducking into alleys occasionally to make out a little, then walking some more, just having a good time. Soon, it was almost six in the morning and time to get home. But first, a fuck.

It was a quick fuck, an easy one. He shoved me up against the wall in an alley and this time, there was no teasing. There was only a bit of anticipation. I panted as he grabbed at my breasts and squeezed them before kissing me hard. I kissed back and wrapped a leg around his body. He pushed his hand down my shirt and I unzipped his pants before stepping quickly out of my panties and pulling my skirt up. Then he fucked me, hard and good. But quick. I came almost instantly because I was so turned on. And then he came. And then it was over and I wanted it again.

"Oh, baby, that was good," I moaned.

"Mmm," he moaned back. "Give me a minute."

I nodded and nibbled at his earlobe and said, "I've got a surprise for you."

"What's that?" he asked and wriggled his eyebrows.

"No," I said, then whispered. "It has nothing to do with a blowjob."

"But you're so good at it."

"Duke," I said and put a finger to his lips. "Shh."

"So what's the surprise?" he asked, smiling slightly.

"I got you a job," I said excitedly.

His smile dropped. "Huh?"

"You're going to do security for our apartment building," I said.

"Like bloody hell I am."

I was taken aback but managed to snap, "Yes, you are."

"No, I'm not," he said, his voice rising. "Nothing I ever do will be good enough for you, will it?"

"Shh, keep your voice down," I said and looked around. No one was around, of course, but still.

"You keep *your* voice down," he snapped.

"I'm just saying, I think you should work."

"No," he said. "You said you got me a job."

I rolled my eyes. "Stop being so huffy. We're out in public. Let's just have a good time and we can argue later."

"Forget it," he said and pulled away from me.

"Duke!" I said. "Come on."

He left me standing there like some imbecile and proceeded out of the alley. I resisted the urge to curse under my breath and followed him out. I did pause to push my skirt down and put my panties in my purse. I found him stopped on the sidewalk, smoking a cigarette, a habit he wouldn't give up for me because "Why should I? It's not going to kill me or anything." It was also a habit I'd obtained from him.

I took the cigarette out of his hand, took a hit and said, "Listen, you have to grow up sometime and that means you have to work."

"I got along quite well before you came along," he said.

My mouth dropped. I was about to rip into him but then I realized, we'd never get along. This was what we were all about—fighting and snappy remarks meant to demean each other, to put each other down. We couldn't get along. We never would be able to. It was doomed. In addition to him being unholy and undead, I was very adamant about certain things. Things like my man working and not being a bum.

"You're an asshole," I said.

"So? You're a bitch."

"Fuck you," I hissed. "All I ask is that you work and—"

"I make money," he said. "In fact, I make more money than you do. What you don't like is that I'm not some stiff wearing a suit working my ass off and being miserable. You think all I do is sit around all day."

"Most days you do!"

"That's because I can," he said. "The real problem, dear Keri, is that you don't like who I am and that includes me being a vampire."

"Well, what's so great about it?" I snapped. "We can't even go out together during the day!"

"Hullo! Sunlight!"

I wanted to slap him so bad. Then I noticed that sun *was* coming up. Good enough for him. I'd love to see him explode right now.

He tapped his foot and pointed up to the sky, which was starting to lighten up. "I mean it—sunlight!"

"I don't give a shit," I said. "I should just let you fry!"

"You'd do that, too, wouldn't you?"

"Yeah, I would."

"You are so cold-hearted!"

"Me?" I screeched. "You don't even have a heartbeat!"

"Yeah, I know," he said. "But I do have a heart, which is more than I can say for you."

"Oh, that's such a good comeback!" I hissed. "What are you going to come up with next? How I don't have a soul?"

He just stared at me. "Maybe you don't."

"You're such a son of a bitch!" I yelled. "How dare you? You're a demon, you're evil and you're calling me soulless?"

"I am."

"Fuck you," I said and rummaged around my purse and pulled out a necklace I'd inherited from my grandmother. So what if it had a cross attached to it? I held it on him.

"What the fuck?" he hissed and jumped away from me. "What are you doing?"

"See? This was my grandmother's necklace and I can't even wear it because of you," I hissed back. "But fuck that now! I'm wearing it."

He stared at me as I put it on, then shook his head and muttered, "This is just like you."

"That's right," I said. "You can't come near me with this on."

"Maybe I don't want to come near you!"

"Oh, you do," I snapped and started to walk off. "I'm going home and you can stand right there and blow up!"

Of course he followed me into the parking garage. (I guess he had to get out of the sun.) Even so, we argued all the way to the car. He told me I was being infantile and I called him a bastard. Then he called me a stupid bint or something and that really pissed me off. I was about to slap him when he grabbed my arm and told me if I didn't stop, he'd have to spank me, which infuriated me.

"Fuck you!" I screamed. "And let go of my arm!"

He shook his head.

"I mean it," I said and jerked my arm away from him. Then I noticed he was staring at me, in that way. "What is it?"

"You look so hot right now," he muttered. "Take off that necklace."

"Fuck off," I snapped but took it off. "I just took it off so nothing will happen to it, not because I want you or anything."

"Right," he said eying me. "So you wanna fuck now or not?"

"Are you out of your mind?" I asked and looked around the deserted parking garage.

"No," he said. "But you are. And you are sexy as hell when you're like that."

I rolled my eyes. "Whatever. I'm leaving."

He grabbed me and kissed me hard, thrusting his tongue into my mouth. I swatted at him but he bent me over someone's car and kept at me until I responded.

I pushed him back and nodded. "Okay, but once we're done, we're getting a divorce."

"Fine," he said and his tone then changed. "I want you so bad. I want to fuck your brains out."

I looked at him and felt a surge of power. I dared him, "So do it."

He grinned and grabbed me, pulling me into his arms. I jumped into them and wrapped my legs around his waist. He pushed me back on the hood of the car, climbing on top of me as he did so. I went with him and soon he was kissing every single square inch of my body. I ached for his mouth to touch—just touch—my nipple. I wanted it so badly, I couldn't stand it. I wanted him and I wanted to be naked beneath him. And I wanted it *now.*

He squeezed my breast and sucked at my neck. I grabbed his head and pushed my mouth on top of his. We kissed with fevered passion as he pushed my shirt up and then he bent to suck my nipple into his mouth. I threw my head back and moaned loudly. That felt so good. His mouth was greedy as he sucked at my nipple. I ran my hands through his hair and never wanted him to stop.

"I'm ready," I moaned. "I want you."

I didn't have to tell him twice. His pants were unzipped and, after he reached up my skirt and played with me, he pushed his hard cock into me, thrusting into me. That's how turned on he was. It was nice to know I elicited that sort of reaction. It's like he had to have me and couldn't wait until he could.

We started kissing, eating at each other's mouths. I couldn't get enough of that kiss, of him, of his cock. He couldn't get enough of me and bent down to suck at my nipple as he fucked me.

For an instant, I wondered if anyone was watching us. But then I didn't care. I was too into it to care. I wanted him and he wanted me. There wasn't anything anyone could do about it, really.

It didn't take any time for us to come. I found myself grinding against him, getting all I could out of the fuck before the orgasm. But it came at me rather quickly and at Duke. Then it was over for us. We kept kissing before we pulled apart and he helped me off the car.

I pushed my skirt down and adjusted my top. He stared at me. I asked, "What is it?"

"I just love you so much, Keri," he said. "I want you to know."

"I thought we were going to get a divorce," I said and smiled at him.

"You didn't mean that," he muttered. "Did you?"

"No, I didn't," I said and hugged him. "Let's not fight anymore, okay? Let's put this behind us and let's just be with each other. Marriage is hard, but we can get through it if we both try."

He nodded.

"Oh, one more thing, Duke," I said.
"What?" he asked and smiled at me.
"Your fly's undone."

✯ ✯ ✯ ✯ ✯

The next day, I had a break from my usual hectic workday, so I had time to sit at my desk and make a list of all the good and bad things about marriage. And about being married to a vampire.

Good things about being married to a vampire:
- ✓ The sex is out of this world.
- ✓ He can make me laugh, sometimes. Well, when he isn't getting on my nerves, which he does most of the time. (Scratch this one.)
- ✓ I don't have to deal with an annoying mother-in-law.
- ✓ The sex is good.
- ✓ I've taken care of the bad clothes thing.
- ✓ He gives really good head. Knows how to suck. (Again, the sex.)

"Ugh!" I groaned and threw the pen down. I couldn't win. I would have to break it off with him. He should have never lied to me! Well, he didn't lie, he just withheld information. He should have told me at first that he was a bloodsucker, then I would have run away from him as any smart girl would have. It wasn't fair what he did. He victimized me. I had let him do it, but still.

It would never work. It wasn't working. Since vampires are sterile, I couldn't have a baby with him but not only that, I couldn't even get a dog. I'd bought this cute little puppy and took it home a few months ago. As soon as I got there, he jumped off the couch and backed away from me—and the puppy.

"Honey," I had said. "Look, I got us a puppy!"

"You got a dog?" he asked and looked terrified.

"Well, you said we couldn't have a kid."

"That doesn't mean for you to go get one of those things," he said and eyed it. It barked at him. "See?"

I stared at the puppy. "What's the problem?"

"I hate dogs and dogs hate me."

"He doesn't hate you," I said and held the puppy out to him. "He doesn't even know you. So, hold him and make friends."

He stared nervously at the dog and then back at me and then tried to take him from me. But, before he got close, the dog went off and I mean this brat started barking and going crazy.

"See!" he yelled and moved away from the barking puppy. "Dogs and vamps don't mix!"

"Oh, come on," I said and soothed the puppy by rubbing his head. "He loves you."

"He? You got a boy?"

"So?"

"Oh, that's even better," he said and shook his head like he was agitated as hell. And he was.

"What do you mean?"

"I mean, boys are more aggressive than girls, obviously."

"Oh."

"Yeah," he said. "But seriously, baby, you have to get rid of that thing."

We got into a big fight over it but I eventually conceded. It was either Duke or the puppy, so it was the puppy. That wasn't fair. It had been a really cute puppy.

I thought about it as I listened to the soft hum of the office. It was lunchtime and everyone was out besides me. I didn't take long lunches. I took short lunches, grabbing stuff on the go as I went to show a house. I took short lunches because I wanted to run home to Duke.

Duke, Duke, Duke. I did love that son of a bitch, even though I couldn't stand him at times. He was good to me. The sex was great. Marriage wasn't so bad. Well, it had sucked so far but maybe it would get better. Maybe we would grow into each other more. We just got started off on the wrong foot. However, if he had told me he was a vamp right off the bat, I would have never slept with him. But because he didn't, and I did, now it was too hard to break it off.

Damn the sex anyway.

"I was a terrible vampire," he told me right after we met. "I didn't have a heart for it. I hated to kill people and once, this old vampire dude asked me if I'd like to share a baby. A baby! Oh, man, that was the worst."

"You're not just telling me this so I won't think you're evil, are you?" I had asked.

He almost cracked a smile and then said, "It's not working, is it?"

I rolled my eyes.

"But I changed," he said he said and grabbed my middle. "Because of you."

"It can't be that easy," I said. "You still don't have a soul."

"What's a soul?" he asked offhandedly. "It's a conscience, that's all it is. Now that I love you, I don't want to do that stuff anymore. My conscience took over."

I felt all warm and glowy inside.

"Besides," he said. "I got a hold of a bloody crackhead once and I can just tell you that was not pleasant. I was up all day coming down off that shit."

I just stared at him.

"But then again, they're almost dead anyway, crackheads," he said and yawned. "And they steal from old ladies."

"You don't…" I began but stopped.

"What?"

"Are you trying to tell me you still eat crackheads or something?"

His mouth dropped, then he said hurriedly, "No, I don't do that. I mean, but if you want an easy… I mean… No. *No.* I don't eat crackheads. But they do steal from old ladies."

"You're lying to me," I said and pointed at him. "You still go to crackdens and eat crackheads, don't you?"

"Not in a while," he said but looked guilty. "I mean, they're almost dead anyway. They're going to OD. And they steal from old ladies."

"Oh, so they don't deserve to live, do they?" I said. "They're about to die anyway *and* they steal from old ladies."

"I don't understand," he said. "Are you setting me up?"

I groaned and said, "I can't believe I married a vampire! I really married a vampire! What kind of idiot am I?"

"But they're almost dead," he said. "That makes it okay. They're going to die anyway and I just…"

"You just help them along?"

"Right," he said and nodded. "And that makes it okay."

"No, it doesn't make it okay, Duke," I said. "I'm sorry, but that doesn't make it okay."

"Either way, they're headed to the great unknown anyway."

I groaned. That's what vampires do—they rationalize death. Crackheads steal from old ladies—off with their heads! Actually, they just suck them dry.

Oh, shit. I put my head on my desk. This was too much to ask of a person. Marriage was hard enough without having to hear about your husband's former kills. We weren't meant to be, Duke and me. We just weren't meant to be. He was a killer and I wasn't. It depressed me but it was true. He was a creature of the night and I was a simple girl, just trying to make it on her own.

I sat up and decided to leave work early. In fact, I was going to go shopping. I deserved something for all my hard work. I didn't drink that much and I only smoked a few cigarettes a day, so I could medicate myself with buying things. Sure, why not?

I grabbed my purse and headed out, almost running to my car. I hadn't been shopping in weeks. The mall was only a few minutes drive from my office and I, luckily, didn't get stopped in any traffic. Still, I drove like a bat out of hell to get there.

I pulled into the mall parking lot, my tires screeching on the asphalt. Oh, hello, new clothes! I would buy a new wardrobe and then I'd divorce Duke and start a whole new life! Or I could stake him in his sleep. Divorces were so messy nowadays and he could even try to get alimony or something. And knowing that he would never remarry, I'd have to pay for that son of a bitch the rest of my life.

"How would you like to pay for that?" the salesclerk asked.

"Credit," I said and handed her my card. Then I shopped the afternoon away, accumulating more and more bags of great stuff. Soon, it was past six and getting dark outside so I decided to head home.

Back at the apartment, I stared at all the clothes and got a sick feeling in the pit of my stomach. I was in so much trouble. I had overspent once again. Now what was I going to do?

The door opened and slammed. Duke was home. *Hurry! Put it all up! Hide it!* Why was I hurrying? Oh, because he'd kill me if he knew I overspent. But then again, it was my money and just a little of his.

I just sat there, though, and waited for him. He came into the bedroom and stared at me, then at all the clothes.

"Did you do it again?" he asked.

I nodded feebly.

"Shit," he said. "Give me the keys to the car. Maybe I can take it all back before the stores close."

"Thank you, honey," I said and smiled at him.

He nodded and gathered up all the clothes and then kissed my cheek before he left. That was another good thing about being married to a vampire—they don't get embarrassed and can return things for you. I was definitely never going to divorce him. *Ever.* What had I been thinking? This was what marriage was all about—your husband bailing you out of crisis. He was the best. I'd give him a good blowjob as soon as he got home.

In case of emergency.

I was meeting my best friend Claire for lunch. She's the girl I was out with the night I met Duke but hadn't seen much of since I'd gotten married, mainly because she doesn't keep vampire hours. Nevertheless, I was preparing myself to ask her for a big favor which included stealing blood from the hospital where she worked. See, I had to do this occasionally as my wifely duty.

Case in point: Once, right after we got married, I cut myself shaving. I cursed and started to wipe it off with a washcloth but then I felt Duke's presence. I stared up at him and smiled and he stared at me, concentrating on the blood on my leg. I could feel his mouth watering.

Not really thinking anything, I said, "You can lick it."

He came over and bent down to my leg without a word and then he licked the blood off. I smiled at him and ruffled his hair. He didn't move away like I expected him too. Before I knew what he was doing, he was sucking on my leg, sucking the blood right out of me. He did it so quickly, I almost passed out. What I had wanted to be an erotic moment led into something really dark. And kinda nasty.

It was like he couldn't stop sucking me and then suddenly he pulled away, stared at me wild-eyed and ran out of the apartment. I didn't see him for three days.

When he showed up again, I was fuming, of course, but then he did something odd. He started packing his suitcase. I was like, "What the hell are you doing?"

"This isn't going to work," he said.

"What?"

"I can't live here with you," he told me and then went back to packing.

I was aghast. "*You're* leaving *me?*"

"I can't do it!" he said and dramatically waved his arms around. "If you bleed, I get hungry!"

"What about when I get my period?" I asked.

"Ugh," he said and slapped himself on the head. "That's not the same thing! Jesus, Keri! It's not an open fucking wound."

"Well, it feels like one!"

"Please," he said. "Don't ever mention that again."

I rolled my eyes. He might have been a creature of the darkness but he was just like all other men and that meant he wanted to know nothing about menses or any other female "problem".

"Listen," he said and bent down, grabbing me by the shoulders. "I will eat you, okay? If this happens again, I will probably end up eating you."

He was being really serious. I couldn't help but crack up. I laughed so hard, my belly started hurting.

He pushed me away. "See? You never take me seriously!"

"Oh, I'm taking you seriously," I said and tried to stop laughing.

"I just can't do this."

"Yes, you can," I said and went to him and put my arms around his waist. "I just won't shave around you anymore. In fact, I'll start getting waxes."

He stared down at me and shook his head. "It's too risky."

"You're not evil anymore, honey," I said. "You're just panicking."

"I know," he said. "But if I hurt you, I wouldn't be able to live with myself."

"You're not alive," I said.

"Stop being a smartass, please."

I grinned up at him and said, "Okay. You're not going anywhere and I will be extra careful from now on."

"I don't want to put you in danger."

"I can take care of myself and, if push comes to shove, I can stake you."

"Promise?" he asked. "Promise to stake me if I do something like that to you?"

"I promise," I said and smiled at him.

He relaxed and said, "If it happens again, though, I am out of here."

"Okay," I said. "Duke, one more question."

"What?"

"Did I taste good?" I asked and rolled with laughter.

He turned paler than normal and just ignored me.

So, instead of breaking up right then and there—or staking him—I decided to try to get him some human blood. So, I did. And, boy, it really did the trick.

"No," Claire said, shaking her head.

"Come on!" I wailed, getting a few looks from people at the busy café where we were having lunch.

"No," she said, shaking her head adamantly.

"Listen to me," I said. "It's his birthday and I don't know what to get him…"

"No," she said.

"Come on," I said. "It's not like—"

"The blood is for people who are dying!"

"He's already dead!" I exclaimed. "He needs it more than anyone else! Help him out, Claire!"

"Why do you do this to me?" she asked. "A month ago it was Valentines and then some stupid anniversary you made up just so I would steal blood from the hospital. I could lose my job!"

"I know," I said. "I'm sorry."

"He could steal it easier from a blood bank," she said.

"But he needs the good stuff," I said. "Blood banks get a lot of their blood from drug addicts and winos."

She just stared at me.

"Come on," I said. "Please?"

"I don't know, Keri."

"Please," I begged. "Please do it for me."

"Why? I mean, what benefit is it of to me?"

"None, really," I said. "But it helps me, your friend."

She just stared at me.

"If I tell you, please don't think I'm weird," I said.

"Oh," she said. "I would never think that. I mean my best friend marries a guy who *thinks* he's a vampire and—"

"Uh, Claire, he *is* a vampire," I said and shook my head at her. After all this time, she still had doubts about Duke. I think she wanted to think that I was into some weird, kinky sex instead of believing the truth. Which, yeah, I could have gone for the weird, kinky sex, but that wasn't what this was about. I added, "And I'm not weird."

"Oh, okay," she said. "Whatever. And, so, when you found out he was, indeed, one of the walking dead, you stayed married to him. No, you're not weird at all."

"He's not one of the walking dead," I scoffed. "Those guys are zombies and they stink to high heaven. *He's* just a vampire."

She just stared at me then hissed, "He's not normal! Is this the way you imagined your life would turn out?"

Well, no, but that was beside the point.

"I mean, is it *that* hard to get a man these days?" she said, shaking her head. "I mean, where are all the good men? Where?!"

"Uh, you need to calm the fuck down," I said. "This isn't about your bad boyfriends."

"You're right," she said. "But I can't do it. I can't get you the blood."

"Please," I said and leaned in. "It's not really for him. It's for me."

She leaned back and studied me. "Did he turn you or something?"

"No," I said. "And I'm out in the daylight."

She raised one eyebrow.

"It's like this, when he gets real blood, he gets real…really… He's something else when he gets it."

She shook her head, not understanding. "I don't know what the fuck you're talking about."

I leaned in towards her and whispered, "His dick gets so hard I can ride it all fucking night."

"Yuck!" she screeched. "How could you… I mean…*ick.* Yuck! Why would you say that to me?"

"Oh, it's not yuck, honey," I said and nodded knowingly.

She considered. "Maybe I should get a vampire."

"I could introduce you to a few."

"I'm not that desperate," she said and shook her head. "Yet."

I nodded.

"Check with me in a few months, though."

I smiled. "So will you do it?"

She eyed me. "Just this once, then stop asking me. I mean it!"

I nodded. I wouldn't ask her again. At least not until our anniversary came up.

★ ★ ★ ★ ★

A few days later, Claire called me and said, "Meet me at my apartment around seven tonight."

So I did. As soon as she opened her front door, I asked, "Did you get it?"

She grinned and handed me a bag of human blood. "No one saw me take it."

"Good," I said and grinned. "Duke is so going to be psyched over this!"

"I went to a lot of trouble over that. I could get fired over it," she said. "Make sure to tell him."

"I will!" I squealed and kissed her cheek. "Gotta go!"

I left hurriedly and drove home. When I got there, Duke was on the couch playing video games. I put the bag of blood behind my back and said, "I got you something."

"Sweetheart, please move for a second," he said, intently playing a video game.

"Duke!" I said. "I got something special for you."

"What is it?" he asked, still playing the damned game.

Oh, hell I couldn't stand the wait any longer. I stomped over, took the game control out of his hand and then tossed the bag at him. He grabbed it and his mouth fell open.

"No way!" he exclaimed. "Did you really?"

"Yup," I said and grinned. "Claire got it for you."

"I love Claire," he said and stood and came over to me. "And I love you more!"

I let him kiss me for a long moment. Damn, he was such a good kisser. He pulled back and we smiled at each other.

"Let me put it up," he said excitedly.

"Put it up?"

"Yeah, I don't want it to spoil," he said and hurried into the kitchen.

Did that just happen or was I in the *Twilight Zone* or something? I shook myself and followed him in. He was just closing the refrigerator door when I entered. "But I thought—"

"What do you want to eat tonight?" he asked.

"What?" I asked.

"I'm starving," he said. "I really want a steak right now."

"But...but—"

He kissed me and said, "Let's eat then I'll drink it."

I glared at him.

He went to the refrigerator and took out two steaks. I watched him, getting more and more annoyed, then told him I'd fix the food.

"Thanks, baby," he said and went back into the living room. I heard the video game come back on.

Fucking hell! Did he just choose that game over me? Over sex? What was this about? I stomped into the living room and said, "I thought I got you the blood for a reason, Duke."

"Keri," he said. "I just wanted to finish this game."

I just stared at him.

"Give me fifteen minutes," he said. "That's all I need."

The audacity! I glared at him, turned on my heel and went back into the kitchen and threw the steaks in a frying pan. I cooked them until they were almost burnt, then called him in to eat. He sat at the table and waited. I grabbed two plates, tossed them on the table, then I slammed the steak on his plate.

He stared at it. "You fried it? It's almost burnt to a crisp. You know I like mine rare."

"Eat it," I said.

"No way," he said.

"Eat it," I said. "It's fine."

"No, it's not," he said and got up from the table and went to the fridge where he pulled out an uncooked steak. "Like so." He slammed the steak down on the plate.

I glared at him.

"Why are you so angry?" he asked and sat down to eat the raw steak.

"I went to a lot of trouble for that blood," I said. "And you're acting all nonchalant over it."

"Sorry," he said. "I just wanted to save it for later."

"Bullshit," I said, getting even angrier. "You can't do anything right. Ever!"

"Yes, I can," he said. "You just don't appreciate me."

My face burned. That's what my mother always told me. "You don't appreciate Duke!" Blah, blah, blah. Well fuck her and fuck him. I was fed up.

"I'll show you how right you are," I said and took off to the bedroom where I opened my nightstand drawer and pulled out a wooden stake. Duke had bought it for me "in case of emergency". There was also some garlic and holy water. This was as good an emergency as any. I went back out with it. He wasn't in the kitchen. I went into the living room and there I tried to stake him as he sat on the couch fuming.

He threw me off him and shook his head. "Woman, I'm warning you!"

"You're worthless!" I yelled and threw the stake at him. "Worthless!"

He grabbed the stake and said, "You wanna stake me?"

"Yes, I do!"

"Fine!" he yelled and held the stake to his heart. "I'll do it! I swear to God, I'll do it!"

"DO IT!" I screamed.

He held it up and then drove it towards his heart. I waited, holding my breath. He stopped and threw it to the side. "I can't do it."

I picked it up and ran at him. "Let me!"

"No," he said and held me off. "I mean it, stop."

But I was going to do it. He was too old for me anyway! I tried to jab him and then the next thing I knew, I was flying through the air and over the couch. I landed next to the bookshelf. I wasn't hurt but I was pissed off.

"You wife beater!" I screamed.

"Oh, shit, are you okay?" he asked and ran to me.

I slapped him. "I hate you."

He pulled back and stared at me. "What is wrong with you?"

I swatted at him feebly and burst into tears. I sobbed on his shoulder, "I just wanted a night of hot sex and you acted like you didn't care."

"I do care, baby," he said and stroked my hair. "I just got busy with my stupid game."

"I know," I said, crying. "You suck!"

"I know I do," he said and kissed my cheek. "I'm a bastard sometimes."

"You are," I said and cried harder, clinging to him. "I just wanted it to be perfect tonight."

"It's perfect every night," he said and smoothed the hair back from my eyes. "You know that."

"I know," I cried and nodded.

"Shh, baby," he said softly.

I sniffled and he kissed my cheek and held me tight. I hugged him back and wondered why we fought so violently, so viciously? Ah, hell, what did it matter?

"How sweet," a disembodied voice came.

"Oh, shit," Duke muttered.

Then there she was. She came into the room in a mist before she finally emerged as a vampire. Her name was Miranda and she was Duke's ex-girlfriend who liked to "drop in" occasionally. I hated her with a passion, especially because she still loved him. I had told her a million times that he was mine, that she was a bitch and should stay away. But she never did. She was always dropping in at the most inopportune times.

"Got any of that blood left for me?" she asked sweetly.

"Get out," I growled.

She shook her finger at me, then turned to Duke. "I'm serious, Duke, I haven't eaten all day."

"Sure," he said and got up.

I glared at her and she glared back. I snapped, "What the fuck do you want?"

"Just stopped in to see my friend," she said and sat on the couch. "How are you, Keri?"

I didn't answer. I got up, grabbed the wooden stake and tried to kill her. She laughed a little, as if this amused her oh, so much, then she had me turned around and her teeth came down to my throat just as Duke cleared his. She stopped but still gave me a little bite that stung just enough to irritate me even further.

"Oh, there you are, love," she said in her fake sounding English accent. "Did you get the blood?"

"Yes," he said. "What are you doing to her, Miranda?"

"Just having a little dinner," she said and smiled sweetly at him. "Come on, let's eat her. You know you want to."

"No, I do not," he said and held out a cup of the blood. "Here. Now let her go."

She dropped me and I fell to the floor. I glared at her and wanted to kill her. But she was much stronger than I was and would have kicked my ass and eaten me. So I really couldn't attempt anything. I hated that.

"You bitch," I hissed at her and held my neck. "She bit me!"

Duke looked at my neck and turned to Miranda. "Next time you do that, I'm taking you out."

"Oh, come on, Duke," she said. "We go way back."

Yeah. They went out for, like, fifty years but that's not that long in vampire years. That's like a couple of weeks. And she was always after him even after he dumped her. He even moved back home to England to get away from her. Or so he told me.

She turned to me. "And how have you been?"

"Get the fuck out of my house," I said then stared at her closely. She had changed her hair, once again. Now it was all black with two gray streaks that came down the sides of her face. I smirked and said, "I see that time has caught up with you."

"I went gray," she said and gave me a knowing look while raising an eyebrow. "By choice."

"God! I hate you so much!" I yelled. "Now get out of here!"

"You invited me in once," she said. "I don't have to leave."

"Duke!" I yelled and glared at him. "Get her out of here!"

She plopped on the couch and grinned at us as she sipped her blood, the blood I'd gotten for Duke and Duke only. I hated her so much. I wished I could have killed her. I tried once. I tried and she beat the shit out of me but not before I pulled some of the stringy—then blond—hair out of her head. She'd vowed revenge ever since. The last time she came while I was sleeping, as I do sleep at night and things like her don't. Duke didn't wake me and let her in and I heard them talking. She had asked him, "What's so special about that bitch anyway?"

He said, "Well, for one thing, she's nothing like you."

Damn right I wasn't! I couldn't help but grin like a fool.

"But what if she accidentally...you know, gets bitten one day?" she asked.

"Let me tell you one thing, Miranda, if you touch one hair on her head, I will hunt you down and kill you. No questions asked."

I so loved him after he said that. I wished he do it anyway. She was always showing up and acting like a bitch. Just as she was acting like a bitch now.

"What brings you here?" Duke asked.

She shrugged. "Going to hook up with some old friends. Thought while I was in town I'd drop in and see how you were and if you'd broken up with that thing."

I grabbed the stake. "I'm going to kill you."

She eyed me without an ounce of fear and said, "Try it once and you will go down. Duke or no Duke."

She wasn't kidding. She was an evil bitch, though. I put the stake down.

"Anyway," she said to Duke, so sickeningly sweet. "I know about this new club that's about to open up and all the vamps in Atlanta are going to be there. You up?"

Duke glanced at me. "How about it, Keri?"

"She doesn't have to come," she said. "We can go alone."

"Fuck you," I said, then yelled at Duke, "She acts like I'm not even in the room! And this is *my* apartment!"

He sighed and said, "We really can't go."

"Neal's going to be there."

His head snapped up. Neal was the first guy he'd ever turned into a vampire. They hadn't seen each other in months, not since we'd had a party at which he tried to have sex with me. He had a thing for me and was always coming onto me. I couldn't take it anymore and threatened to tell Duke about what he was doing. He left without a word and Duke thought he was mad at him. I didn't say anything because... Well, I didn't want to seem like a bitch.

Duke turned to me. "Please?"

I groaned. "Okay, but if that bitch pisses me off, you have to promise to dust her."

"I promise," he said.

"Hey!" Miranda snapped. "I'm sitting right here."

Neal.

The so-called "club" was nothing but an old factory where an assortment of vampires and demons and the like had gathered to have a big party. They were all drinking liquor and beer and God only knows what else. The music was so loud it almost split my eardrums. Miranda, thankfully, disappeared into the crowd as soon as we got there so I didn't have to put up with her. Duke and I wandered around looking for his old pal Neal but we couldn't find him.

"I knew she was lying!" I shouted over the loud music.

"Why would she do that!" Duke shouted back.

"Why does she do anything!" I shouted, shaking my head.

"Huh!" he shouted.

"Nothing," I muttered, then shouted, "Let's get out of here!"

"Okay!" he shouted right in my ear.

"Ow!" I exclaimed and held my hand over my ear.

"Sorry," he mumbled.

It took a good ten minutes to get through the crowd and to the door. Everyone stopped us and shook Duke's hand and asked who I was. When he told them I wasn't a vamp or a demon, they seemed a little disappointed. Some of them seemed a little hungry, so I figured it was time to leave. I almost ran to the door, dragging Duke behind me.

"Thank God," I said as soon as we hit the sidewalk.

"Yeah, that party was boring," he said. "You know, in the good old days, I had some really wild parties."

I just stared at him. He nodded at me and leaned back on his heels as if he were caught up reminiscing to himself. I rolled my eyes and said, "Come on. Let's stop by a diner and have some breakfast or something."

"Yeah, I didn't get any supper," he said.

"Well, that was your own fault," I snapped.

"My fault?" he asked and stopped.

"Yeah," I said. "It was your fault."

"How's that?"

"You were being insensitive to my needs."

He balked. "*I* was being insensitive to *your* needs?"

"Uh, yeah," I said, nodding.

"Keri," he started. "Sometimes you should just let stuff go."

"What the hell does that mean?"

"It means—"

But he was cut off by a piercing scream. And it was coming from a female. It was scream that meant she was about to get bitten. Duke was always on the lookout to help unsuspecting females since we'd been together because he "couldn't bear the thought" of someone biting me. It was his way of giving back some of what he'd taken. I thought it was quite valiant of him, although I suspected that his main motivation was to score points with me.

Duke and I looked at each other for a split second and then ran in her direction. We found the young girl in an alley surround by three vamps. Duke took out two of the guys as I grabbed the girl and pulled her away.

"Are you okay?" I asked her as I dragged her away from the alley.

"What was that?" she asked in whisper.

"Nothing," I said. "Where's your car?"

She pointed and I walked her to it, put her in it, then said, "What the hell are you doing in a place like this at this time of the night?"

"Who are you?" she snapped. "My mother?"

Then she drove off.

I hollered after her, "Well, you're welcome!"

Bitch. I stomped back to the alley, hoping Duke was finished dusting them. I really wanted something to eat. I hadn't eaten since lunch and it was past midnight. Then I wanted to go home and crash. I didn't even know if I was in the mood for sex anymore. I was always up late since I'd met Duke. It was starting to drain me.

As I neared the alley, I heard Duke talking to someone, then laughter. Oh, no. I looked over and of course, it was Neal, the vamp we'd come to see at the party. I was actually disappointed it was him. He was one of the few vampires that Duke had made that hadn't gotten staked. *Yet.* All of the others were apparently just dumb or they got too greedy because most of them had met their demise one by one until this dude was the only one left.

Why didn't someone kill him too already?

"Keri?" Neal asked. "Is that you?"

I hid my groan and said, "Yeah, it's me."

"Wow," he said and smiled at me, consuming me with his eyes. "Come here and give me a hug."

But I didn't want to. I *had* to. So, I let him hug me for a moment and of course he copped a feel of my ass. *Bastard!* If he kept this shit up, I was going to tell Duke about him. I pulled away quickly.

"Honey," Duke said, putting his arm around my waist. "Neal's gonna stay with us tonight."

Oh, fucking shit.

★ ★ ★ ★ ★

After he consumed almost all of the blood I'd gotten for Duke, Neal was content to kick back on our couch and tell us of all his "adventures". He'd been to some foreign country and all this other shit. And that's all it was, too. It was shit. He hadn't ever been out of the States. How was he going to travel overseas? He couldn't take a plane or a ship. And that's because he was always broke and constantly bumming money.

"Wow," Duke said. "That sounds really cool."

No, it *sounded* like bullshit.

"What do you think, honey?" Duke asked, turning to me.

"I think it's great," I said. "Bolivia, huh? Isn't that were they have all those diamond mines?"

Neal studied me for a moment before saying, "Uh, I don't know."

"Want some more wine?" Duke asked and stood.

"Sure," Neal said and handed him his glass.

Duke took it, then asked me, "How about you, honey?"

"I'm fine," I said and smiled at him.

A soon as he was gone, Neal turned to me and said, "You don't like me, do you?"

"Was there ever a question of that?" I asked.

He grinned. "Why not? Why not like me?"

"Because every time you come around, you stir up shit," I said. "Why are you here this time?"

"Just dropped in to see some old friends."

"That's what Miranda said," I said.

"Oh, is she here?"

I rolled my eyes.

"You know, she's still in love with Duke," he told me.

"I know," I said. "Otherwise, she wouldn't drop in all the time and throw herself at him."

He nodded. "Keri, I've been thinking about something."

"What is it?"

He scooted closer to me and whispered, "I just want you to know that I think I'm in love with you."

I rolled my eyes and set him straight, "No, you're not."

"I'm not?"

I shook my head. "No, you're not in love with me. You're just jealous that Duke is having some sort of normal life and you can't stand for him to be happy."

He thought about it. "Wow, I think you're right."

"Stop trying to mess with us," I said. "Go find someone and live your own life."

He nodded. "Maybe I will."

"I think you should," I said and stood up just as Duke came back into the room. "I think I'm going to bed."

"So soon?" Duke asked.

I nodded. "Yeah, it's early, I know, being almost four in the morning, but I need a few hours' sleep before work."

"Okay, honey," Duke said and kissed my cheek. "Goodnight."

"Night," I said.

As soon as I was in bed, I heard them talking. They were discussing something that happened at the turn of the century. I stared at the ceiling and asked, "Why did I marry a vampire?"

Second wind.

I left work later than usual and was just about to call Duke to tell him I'd be home late when my cell phone rang. It was Neal and he wanted to see me.

"Sorry," I said. "I have to get home."

"I'd really like to see you, though," he said.

I rolled my eyes. "What is this about?"

"I was thinking of the stuff you said last night," he said. "Obviously, I don't want Duke to know or anything, but I'd like to talk some more about it. If you could do that for me, I'd really appreciate it."

"Whatever," I said. "But I can't do it tonight. I'm beat from work."

"How about tomorrow?"

"Okay," I said. "Where?"

"There's this little restaurant called Phil's and it's on—"

"I know where it's at," I said. "What time?"

"Around eight?"

"I'll see what I can do," I said.

"Thanks, Keri," he said. "You're the best."

"Sure," I said and hung up and threw my cell into the passenger seat. Oh, shit, I needed to call Duke. I picked it up and started to call, but then decided against it. I was almost home anyway.

I sighed. Damn, I was so tired. No more late nights for a while. Maybe I was getting old, needing my sleep. Regardless, I couldn't do this anymore. We'd been up late every night this week and it was starting to wear on me. I was going home, getting in the tub and soaking for a good half-hour. Then I wanted a full body massage and some sex, then sleep.

Sounded like a plan to me.

I pulled into the parking garage a few minutes later, grabbed my bag and got on the elevator. God, I was so tired. I needed my second wind so bad. As I opened the front door, I called, "Duke, you are going to have to give me a back massage."

No answer.

"Duke?" I said and looked around. He wasn't in the living room. I knew he was home because the video game he'd been playing was paused on the TV. I threw my keys and bag on the coffee table and bent to pick up the remote, then I heard something. I straightened up and listened. It was Miranda. She was talking...no, she wasn't talking, she was...

Oh, God, please don't let this be happening!

Just in case I was wrong, and because I didn't want to look like a fool, I crept silently into the bedroom. Unfortunately, I wasn't wrong. I was right. Miranda and Duke were having sex.

I closed my eyes and felt my heart drop to my knees where it shattered into a million tiny pieces. I wanted to fall to the floor and die. How could this be happening to me?

Why was it happening to me? What did I ever do to deserve it?

Oh, fuck. This wasn't my plan! My plan had been to come home and crash! And they'd ruined it!

Just then, Miranda threw her head back and moaned, "Duke!"

Suddenly, I had the second wind I'd needed earlier and it was fueled by rage. I was going to kill her! How dare she say his name like that? Oh, I was going to kill her! Now!

The stake. Where was it? It was still in the living room. I raced back out and grabbed it, then ran back in there and... Dear God, they were still at it! Before I could stop myself, I pushed Duke off her and jumped on top of her and was just about to drive the stake in when she vanished. I ended up staking my new mattress.

Duke muttered, "How did she do that?!"

I turned on him. "You motherfuckingsonofabitch!"

He jumped off the bed from me and backed away from me.

I stalked him, holding the stake. "You're going to die now!"

"Keri, listen to me," He said, holding up his hands, palms facing. "I can explain this."

"No need to explain," I growled and glared at him. "I hate you so much."

"Listen—"

I wasn't about to. I was a scorned woman, for God's sake! And he was going to pay. I ran at him but he managed to grab the stake and ward me off. Fine! I ran to the nightstand and grabbed the holy water and threw it at him.

He dodged it and screeched, "Stop that!"

I threw it again. This time it landed on his skin and boiled and hissed. Good enough. He reached over and, in a second flat, had the bottle and threw it against the wall.

Garlic. My next plan of attack.

"Nooo!" he hissed. "I hate the smell of garlic!"

I swung it around. "Don't like it, huh? Should have thought about that when you were sleeping with that skanky ho! How can I ever let you touch me after *that*?"

"Keri, let me explain," he said.

"Explain what?" I asked and burst into tears. "Explain that while I was out busting my ass to give us a better life you were fucking that whore?"

His head dropped.

I fell down and sobbed, "How could you do that to me?"

"I am so sorry," he said. "It didn't mean anything."

"Does it not mean anything when we do it, too?"

"Oh, baby," he said. "Of course it does."

He tried to take me in his arms but I pulled away and stood. "I can't stand to look at you right now."

He dropped his head and looked really sad. But I didn't care. I was hurting so bad I couldn't care.

"Listen," he said. "She tricked me."

"Oh, come on," I snarled. "So she tricked you into putting your dick in her pussy? How's that happen?"

"She just kept coming on to me and then I think she slipped something in my drink and—"

"Shut up!" I screamed at him. "I can't take it anymore."

He stared at me numbly.

"I can't take it," I said and began to sob even more. I beat on my chest and said, "The pain, it hurts so bad."

"That just means you're alive, baby."

"Then kill me!" I screamed.

"No, I can't do that."

"You pussy!"

"You can say anything you want to me," he said quietly. "But you'll never convince me to hurt you ever. I'll never do it."

"If I could kill you right now, I would," I said. "And why her? You know how much I hate her!"

"She tricked me!" he roared. "I know that sounds like bullshit but she tricked me. She came over here with a bottle of wine and the next thing I know, we're... *That.* I know she got some potion from a witch or somebody but I didn't realize it until a moment before you came into the room."

"Bullshit!" I yelled.

"I'm not lying," he said.

"No, but you're leaving," I said and pointed to the door. "Get out."

"Keri, come on," he sad. "You have to believe me."

I shook my head. "No, I don't, Duke."

He stared at me as if he couldn't believe I'd just said that. But I had and I couldn't take it back. He nodded at me once then left, quietly. As soon as the front door closed, I fell to the floor and began to cry. I didn't stop for the longest time.

Before Duke.

I called in sick for the next few days. I was over everything—my career, my husband, and my life. That's what having a broken heart does to a girl. It breaks her totally and unconditionally. And I was broken. I didn't think I'd ever get over it. Once I was in that misery that heartbreak brings, I couldn't imagine being any other way. I couldn't imagine being happy or loved. Or feeling sexy. I looked like crap. I didn't take a bath and I had a feeling I was beginning to stink. I didn't care, though. The only person I saw during this time was Claire.

Claire came over and listened to me rant and roar against Duke. She agreed with everything I said, which was always the best friend's job.

I'd been through a lot of breakups before. I'd had about five or six exes. None of them were like this. And, besides, I was never married to any of them. Maybe that's why this was hell. Of course, I'd broken up with every one of them, so that might have been why I hadn't gotten too down about it. And none of them had cheated on me. But still. This was hell. It was like someone had taken a chunk out of my heart and stomped on it, while it was still beating. It was like they had taken part of me away.

Fucking Miranda. I just wished she'd "drop" by. I'd stake her before she could blink. That bitch had ruined my life. She had single-handedly destroyed my marriage. Sure, he was there with her, but it was really her fault. Sure, we had fought and I thought we were an odd couple and not exactly right for each other, but it was my call to make. She forced me to make it. She forced him out of my life and that's because she was a miserable, selfish bitch.

"Women are such bitches," I told Claire as I sipped on a beer.

"You got that right," she said.

"He said she tricked him," I said. "Do you believe that?"

"Anything's possible with those kind of people," she said.

I nodded and stared at the TV, which was turned off. It had been almost a week. Duke hadn't come by or called but I had a feeling he was "watching" me. The bastard. I suddenly got an idea.

"Let's go out!" I exclaimed.

"Why?"

"It'll make me feel better," I said.

She considered, then nodded. "Sure. It'll be like old times, just me and you before Duke."

Before Duke. That made my heart sink. Before Duke was such a... Well, I'd been single and I'd had a blast, but after he'd come into my life, I'd never felt so alive, even if he was dead. But he was so much fun and so charming and once I got him into some nice clothes, he looked great.

"I can't take this," I said and jumped up off the couch. "Let's go."

"Uh, first," she said. "You need to bathe."

"Am I that bad?" I asked and sniffed myself.

"Yeah, you're getting ripe."

✶ ✶ ✶ ✶ ✶

After I showered and put on some body-hugging clothes, Claire and I went out. We hit a good club because there's no better place for a girl trying to mend a broken heart. I began to actually feel happy and we got our groove on with some cute guys on the dancefloor and then we made them buy us drinks.

"I think I might like this guy," Claire said and jerked her head to the cute guy she'd been dancing with all night. "Do you mind if I ditch you?"

"No," I said. "Go for it."

"I will," she said and wriggled her eyebrows.

"Call me," I said.

"Will do," she replied and got up, taking her cute boy out of the club.

I sighed. Well, if nothing else, Claire would get laid and that hadn't happened in a long time. She was so picky. But then again, why should she settle? She was pretty and in great shape and had a good job. She didn't have to settle.

Neither did I. Just then, the guy I'd been dancing with on and off all night came back with our drinks. He was tall and cute, just the way I liked them. I could do him. Hey, why not? I was single again.

"What happened to your friend?" he asked and sat the drinks down.

I shrugged. "Headache."

"Do you have to leave, too?"

"Nah," I said and smiled at him. "Sit down."

He grinned and sat down. He was so not like Duke. He would do for tonight. We'd get it on and then he'd leave. He'd be my…what was it called? Closure? Yeah. That's what he'd be. And I needed closure. I was going to see a lawyer tomorrow.

I scooted in close to him and whispered, "So, tell me a little about yourself."

"You never asked, but my name's John," he said.

I hadn't asked. But what did I need to know his name for? I was just going to use him. I thought about how that sounded. Oh, shit. I sounded like such a bitch. I felt like one, too. I had to get out of there. I knew I'd get him back to my place and not be able to go through with it anyway and there was no sense in ruining his night.

I was about to give him an excuse and leave but then, of course, I saw Duke in the shadows of the club. I rolled my eyes. I hated it when he acted like a vamp in public. What was this shit? Why was he here? I glanced at John. Oh. I knew it! I knew he was following me.

Well, fuck him. I ignored him and got cozy next to John, running my hand along his chest and whispering in his ear. I glanced over at Duke, who was now approaching our table. This ought to be good.

Without a hello, Duke said, "Who's this?"

I didn't reply and took John's hand.

"Who's this?" he asked again and stared at him menacingly.

I smiled at him. I'd play along. Sure, why not? So, I said, "This is John. John this is—"

"The man who is going to smash your face in," he said and bared his teeth. "Now beat it!"

It didn't take John two seconds to come out of his seat and scurry away. I guess I would have, too, but still. What a wuss! I was suddenly glad I hadn't fucked him. I stared at Duke. I was suddenly pissed off. I tried to not let it show. I mean, why give him the satisfaction?

"Duke!" I snapped as I watched John run away. "I liked that guy."

"Well, I didn't."

"You can't do this," I said and grabbed my purse and stood. "You're going to turn into a stalker."

"And I will stalk you forever," he said. "I'm not about to let you get hurt by some asshole like that."

"He's not an asshole, but you are." I started to walk away, but then stopped. "Why? Why are you doing this?"

"You know why."

"I don't," I said. "Tell me!"

"Because I love you!" he roared. "I bloody fucking love you and it eats me up inside and then you go out with some chump like that! Or should I say, chimp?"

I so wanted to slap him. "Don't you say anything about him! You don't know him."

"I don't have to know him!"

"At least I didn't fuck him in our marital bed!"

He blanched. "I figured you'd bring that up."

"Why shouldn't I?" I asked. "And John was my date. I'm going to find him now and then I'm going to fuck him."

"Why?"

"Just because I know it would kill you."

"Well, then I'll kill him first," he said and started to go after John.

I grabbed his arm and shook my head. He reluctantly stopped and turned to me. I decided to play him a little. "Get over it, Duke. He's a good guy and you know nothing about him."

He nodded. "I know he's not right for you."

"And you are?" I scoffed.

"I am."

"You're dead, number one and number two, we are over. *Over!*"

"I know," he said. "But I still love you."

And then he walked away, leaving me standing there feeling like a complete idiot. It was a familiar feeling.

Divorcée.

A few weeks later, I stared at the papers the lawyer had drawn up. This was it. I was going to be a divorcée. A bitter one at that.

I threw them down and began to sob. My life was over. *Over!* I cried for a few minutes, then went into the bathroom and rinsed my face off. As I stared at myself in the mirror, I knew Duke hadn't lied. Miranda had tricked him. I shouldn't have overreacted. I should have listened more, been kinder. But that wasn't like me. I was who I was.

The doorbell rang.

My shoulders slumped but I went to the door and answered it. It was Duke. He was here to sign the papers, just like I'd asked him yesterday when I'd caught him stalking me again.

"Come in," I said.

He walked in and sat on the couch. He didn't say anything.

"Here," I said and handed him the papers. "Sign here."

He nodded and held up the pen. "Here?"

I nodded. Just as he was about to sign it, I grabbed it and said, "I can't do it!"

"Do what?"

"Divorce you," I said. He wasn't the demon. I was. I wasn't acting any better than any of them and, hey, they had an excuse. Some of them were born evil and some of them were turned evil. I was just evil because I was a bitch.

"You're not evil," he said.

"Don't read my mind right now," I said.

"Listen," he said. "We've had a rough time of it. Let's not push it right now."

I nodded.

"You need some time and so do I," he said.

"You need some time?" I asked, feeling a little miffed.

"I do," he said. "Let's hold off on all of this until our emotions settle."

"You're telling me you want some time apart?" I asked.

"I think it would be good for us."

I stared at him, aghast. Here I was ready to beg him to come home when he didn't even want to come home. I had to asked, "Are you seeing Miranda?"

"No," he said slowly. "I've run across her since—"

"I knew it!" I yelled and jumped up. "Just get out of here, Duke! Leave and don't come back!"

He glared at me. "I was here to try and get this thing settled."

"Well, you didn't do a very good job," I hissed. "Now get out!"

He nodded once and said, "You're still pissed off and that's why I want us to take time apart. I want us to get over this before we try and move on."

"Stop watching so many fucking talk-shows," I said. "And don't ever try that psychobabble with me again."

"Fine!" he shouted. "I was just trying to make things better!"

"Well, it's not working!" I said. "You never could make things better and you never will be able to."

"Not with you!"

"Get out!" I screamed.

"Oh, I will," he hissed.

And then he did. He was gone. I felt worse than ever before. I was going out. I was going out right now. I grabbed my purse and nearly ran to the elevator and then to my car. I peeled out of the garage and then down the street. I didn't stop until I got to a club. It was just after nine. No one was there yet. I didn't want to wait. I just wanted to fuck the first guy I met. I was going to get Duke out of my system once and for all.

Almost as soon as I arrived, someone tapped me on the shoulder. It was Neal. He looked sad. He said, "You never met me that night. I waited forever on you."

"You've got time to spare," I said then got an idea. And it was a good one. And it would so piss Duke off, which was the point of it all.

"Huh?" Neal asked. "Did you hear me?"

"Why don't you come back to my place?" I asked, smiling sweetly at him. "We can talk there."

★ ★ ★ ★ ★

"No," Neal said and jumped up off the couch. "No way!"

"Come on," I said. "All you have to do is bite me, I bite you back and it's over."

"It's a little more complicated than that," he said.

"Not really," I said and stood up, pressing myself next to him. "If you do it, I'll let you do anything you want to me."

He eyed me, liking that idea. But then he moved away and said, "I can't. Duke's my best friend."

"He cheated on me with Miranda!"

"Yeah, but she tricked him," he said. "She really tricked him. That wasn't Duke having sex with her. That was Duke on drugs."

I stared at him. "What the hell does that mean?"

"It means, she tricked him," he said. "She pulled some witchy shit on him."

"Whatever," I said, then smiled at him. "Come on, Neal. What's the big deal? Haven't you turned anyone before?"

"Well, yeah," he said. "But they weren't desperate like you."

"I'm not desperate," I said, almost affronted. "Come on!"

He shook his head.

I decided to try another approach. I went to him, pulled his lips on top of mine and kissed him as hard as I could. I pulled back first and said, "Anything you want to do. *Anything.*"

He was breathless. He was hot with lust for me. I was going to get him to do it. I smiled with satisfaction.

"Okay," he said. "But you have to know it hurts."

"Whatever," I said.

He did it. He did it because he said he loved me. Too bad I loved Duke. And it was painful, more painful than I could have ever imagined. He pulled my head back and sank his teeth into my neck, which hurt, then he began to suck at my neck. I almost blacked out. I began to fall to the floor, but he held me up and kept consuming me. I was to the point of no return, almost there. I was about to die. When was he going to stop sucking my blood?

Just then, he was thrown off me and Duke was beating the shit out of him. I stood there and held my bleeding neck and then I fell to the floor.

"Man, I told her I didn't want to do it!" Neal yelled, trying to fend Duke off.

Duke didn't answer him and kept beating him. Soon, Neal took off through the door and disappeared. I watched him go but couldn't move. I just lay there and felt so weak, weaker than I'd ever felt.

Duke rushed to me and gathered me up in his arms. I stared into his eyes and saw that love I thought had vanished. But it hadn't vanished. It had always been there. I had just been too stupid to recognize it.

"This is so typical of you," he said, almost on the verge of tears. "Why did you have to do this, baby? All this, turning yourself into a vampire, and for what?"

He hugged me so tight then, as if he'd never let me go. I blinked heavily and I think I blacked out, then I felt it, I felt his blood in my mouth and I began to drink it, to suck at his arm which he'd cut and offered me. I kept sucking at it until he pulled back. Then I blacked out.

Eternity.

Duke was next to the bed watching me sleep. As soon as I opened my eyes, he smiled gently at me.

"Hey," he said.

"Hey," I muttered. "What happened?"

"You're a vamp now," he said. "Welcome to my world."

"Am I really?" I asked and sat up, then my head swam.

"Easy," he said. "Neal almost drained you completely. He lost control."

"Oh," I said.

"Why did you do it?"

"Because of you," I said. "Because I couldn't stand not being with you anymore and I guess… I was just dumb."

He nodded slightly. "It didn't have to end up like that."

"You didn't have to leave me."

"You told me to leave," he said. "Don't you remember?"

I did. I just didn't want to admit it. He was right. I hated it when he was right.

"Now what are you going to do?" he asked. "You can't work during the day and you can't—"

I put my finger to his lips and said, "Don't sweat it, baby."

He smiled at me. "I won't."

"I'm sorry," I said. "I'm sorry for not believing you and I'm sorry for—"

"It's okay," he said, cutting me off. "Let's not talk about it. That's just the way it goes sometimes."

"Yeah," I muttered.

"Think of it this way," he said and climbed into bed with me. "Now we can spend eternity together. Literally."

Oh, shit. I hadn't thought about it like that. Eternity was a long fucking time. I shook myself and changed the subject, "Why am I so weak? I thought I was a vamp and vamps are strong."

He chuckled. "You have to acclimate. You'll be stronger in a few days."

"A few days?" I asked, wrinkling my nose. "But I have to go to work."

"You can't," he said. "You'll have to get a job at a convenience store."

"I am not working there," I said. "Are you serious?"

He nodded. "We probably won't be able to afford this apartment, either. Have to move into a sewer or something."

He had to be out of his damn mind.

"At night, we can go out and hunt," he said. "Are you ready for your first kill, baby?"

I stared at him. Actually, I wasn't ready for my "first kill". I thought about sucking blood and almost felt like throwing up.

"Are you okay?" he asked.

"I feel sick," I said.

"Just lie still. It'll pass."

I lay back and closed my eyes. My head was throbbing. Being a vampire sucked.

"Oh, bloody hell," he muttered. "I can't take it anymore."

I opened my eyes and stared at him. "Take what?"

"You're not a vamp."

"Huh?"

He laughed. "I knew you'd try to get Neal to turn you, so we got a little potion that made you feel like you had been."

My mouth dropped. I did feel a wave of relief sweep over me but then I felt something else—anger. How could he?! I yelled, "You son of a bitch! How long were you going to go on with that crap?"

"As long as I could get away with it," he said and grinned. "I had you going, didn't I?"

I grunted at him and crossed my arms. "Why did you do that?"

"Because I knew you really didn't want to be a vampire," he aid. "But I knew you'd try to get someone to turn you, just to get back at me."

I narrowed my eyes at him. "I'm going to do it now just to spite you!"

"Shh," he said and took my hand. "Baby, I just wanted all this behind us. Why don't you let it go and I'll let it go too?"

I stared at him and muttered, "I guess I could, but that's a cruel joke."

He shrugged. "Well, I am evil."

"You really are," I said.

"That's life, baby," he said. "And that's all it will ever be."

I just stared over at him and then none of it mattered. Here we were, together. I smiled. "But it's a good life to have, Duke."

"As long as I can spend it with you," he said. "It will be."

I grinned at him. He'd finally said something right.